Gypsy
and
Nimblefoot

A HORSE MUST DIE...

unless Wendy can find the source of the terror that turns him into a potential killer whenever it strikes. With only the help of her own beloved horse, Gypsy, Wendy must save the beautiful, gentle Nimblefoot from destruction—but how?

At the same time, Wendy's life is further complicated when she is caught up in eerie goings-on at the abandoned cabin in Gulligan Gulch—the *haunted* gulch.

When the guest season starts at Wendy's aunt and uncle's dude ranch, Jimmy returns—Jimmy, the boy who rode Nimblefoot on the trail ride that resulted in the horse's fall and injury and subsequent frightening behavior. The boy's strange hostility is still another puzzle that Wendy must deal with. Is Jimmy concealing something about the horse's fall, something that might help with Nimblefoot's awful problem?

This is a story of love and trust—between Wendy and Gypsy and Nimblefoot—and courage in the face of death-dealing danger to themselves and others.

Gypsy
and
Nimblefoot

By SHARON WAGNER

Illustrated by Marilyn Hamann

Cover by Jean Helmer

 GOLDEN PRESS

Western Publishing Company, Inc.

Racine, Wisconsin

Contents

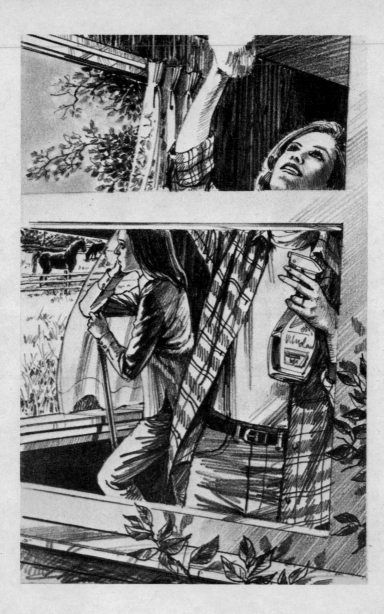

1 · Guests Coming

WENDY LEANED on her broom for a moment, staring off across the deep grass of the home pasture. It was hard to believe that only two weeks had passed since the big blizzard that had nearly brought tragedy to the ranch. Spring had come to Montana with the same suddenness as the snowstorm had.

"We're almost done," Aunt Laura said, "and I do appreciate the help. It's always such a hassle trying to get the cabins ready for the first few guests, and the Websters are even coming early this year."

"What are they like?" Wendy asked, pushing back her long, light brown hair before returning to her sweeping.

Aunt Laura paused in her window polishing. "Mr. and Mrs. Webster are nice, but they really aren't too crazy about the rustic life," she said, her tone telling Wendy that there was more to it.

"Then why do they come?" Wendy asked, remembering all too well her own misgivings about life on a ranch. Though her reasons had had nothing to do with the rustic life, she certainly hadn't wanted to come here to stay with her aunt and uncle while her father accepted an overseas assignment from the company he worked for.

"Their son, Jimmy, is a bit of a problem to them, and his doctor recommended sending him to camp in the summertime to toughen him up. I guess they can't bear to let him out of their sight that long, so they bring him here."

"Sounds like a real brat," Wendy observed without enthusiasm. She'd been looking forward to the beginning of the tourist season—to seeing what it was like when the three guest cabins were full—but now. . . .

"He's not that bad," Aunt Laura said with a soft chuckle. "In fact, he and Art were getting along just fine last year . . . till the accident."

12

"What accident?" Wendy asked. For just a moment she felt the familiar ache in her right knee, a reminder of her own accident—a heartbreaking one that had nearly destroyed her dream of riding and owning a horse of her own.

Aunt Laura looked uneasy, almost as though she didn't want to go on, and Wendy, waiting, shivered slightly, though the late May sun was bright and warm. Had Jimmy done what she had? Had he, too, been foolish and careless, allowing a horse to be hurt or killed?

She thought of Buck and the accident she'd had back in Phoenix, then forced the thoughts away firmly. That was behind her now. She had learned from it and would be more careful because of it; but she couldn't let it keep her from riding and loving horses—not now that she had Gypsy for her very own.

"What happened, Aunt Laura?" Wendy asked, relieved that her voice didn't reveal her thoughts.

"No one is really sure," her aunt said carefully. "Art had been teaching Jimmy to ride, and he was doing well. He'd graduated from old Ladybug to a pony and was finally ready to ride a younger

13

horse. Art had several that were gentle enough for the boy to handle, but Jimmy had his heart set on Nimblefoot."

Again Wendy felt a twinge of sympathy. There had been many other horses at the riding stable, too, but Buck had been her favorite, the only one there that she'd ever wanted to have for her own. A whinny from the corral brought her attention back to the present. Gypsy sounded impatient. She looked at her aunt, anxious for her to finish the story. "So?"

"Jimmy rode him around here for several days, and they really seemed perfectly suited to each other. Then we took the guests on a little trail ride."

"You mean one of the Saddle Club rides?" Wendy asked, thinking about the one that was to be held Saturday. It would be her first, and she was feeling a bit anxious about it.

"No, just a ride here on the ranch, along the north pasture and down to the lake. It's a nice ride, with enough ridges and rough country to be interesting, but not long enough to make the guests too sore to ride again." She paused for a

14

moment, then added, "You'll be going on a dozen of them this summer. Everyone seems to enjoy them."

"But what about Jimmy and Nimblefoot?" Wendy asked, standing back to check over the porch of this last cabin. The cleaning was all done, but she didn't want to mention it till Aunt Laura finished telling her about the accident.

"We don't really know what happened. Something may have frightened Nimblefoot, or Jimmy might have made a mistake, or the horse may have just slipped on a loose rock on the trail, as sometimes happens. An experienced rider would have steadied the horse, but Jimmy was a beginner, and. . . ." She shrugged. "It was a bad fall, worse for the horse than for the boy, though it was a while before the Websters realized that."

Wendy waited for a moment, hoping that her aunt would go on, but finally she had to ask, "What happened to the horse? Did you have to. . . ." She couldn't bring herself to ask the question, remembering her own agony when she learned that Buck had to be destroyed after the accident that put her in the hospital.

15

"Art was afraid that he might have to have the horse destroyed, but Dr. James said that his shoulder was only torn and sprained, not broken. So when he was well enough, we just turned him out with the Appaloosa mares and foals for the summer. In fact, I don't think he's been ridden since the accident."

"What about Jimmy?" Wendy asked, feeling better.

"I don't think he's been on a horse since," Aunt Laura said. "He wasn't really hurt, just bruised and shaken up, but it was near the end of their stay, and the Websters were very upset. They wouldn't even let him go near the corrals."

"Poor kid," Wendy said, remembering her own terror at the thought of endangering another horse by riding it. "Maybe I can help him this year."

Her aunt's smile was warm, but there were reservations in her eyes when she said, "I hope you can, dear. Now, why don't you go down and see what Art's doing? I hear your filly calling you."

"Are we through?" Wendy asked, though she longed to race off to the corrals, where she'd been helping her uncle with the training of the young Appaloosas.

"Yes, thank goodness," Aunt Laura said with a laugh. "Now I can start making a list of the supplies I'll need. I always have trouble adjusting to cooking for so many extra people in the summer. I get all out of practice with just the two hands and us all winter."

"I'll help you," Wendy promised, though she couldn't help wondering if the days were going to be long enough to do everything she'd planned for the summer.

"I know you will," her aunt said, giving her a quick hug. "Now, go tell Art what horse you want for the Saddle Club ride. You've only got today to get ready for it."

Wendy hurried across the corner of the lawn and along the heavily grown pasture to the big corral, where her uncle was working with one of the two-year-olds while the rest of the young horses watched from the smaller second corral. The Morgan filly, Gypsy, whickered a greeting, her one blue eye and one brown eye bright as she tossed her red brown head eagerly.

17

"Think you've got time before lunch to give the yearlings each a turn on the long line?" Uncle Art asked. "I'd like to get finished with all the workouts this morning. Then we can go down to the lake pasture this afternoon and pick out the dude horses we want to use to start the season."

"I'll try," Wendy said. "We just finished up the last cabin, so Aunt Laura hasn't started to cook yet."

"It's going to be a busy summer," Uncle Art said, "and keeping the young horses around to train isn't going to make it any easier, but with your help. . . ."

"I love doing it," Wendy said, hurrying to the corral fence where the long lounge line was hanging. She whistled for Gypsy, though it wasn't necessary, for the filly was waiting at the gate, eager to be first.

Wendy snapped the line to the filly's halter, then picked up the long training whip. She was proud of the way Gypsy trotted out to the full length of the line and then stopped, her ears pricked up, waiting for Wendy's first command.

"Walk, Gypsy," Wendy said, then tried to con-

18

trol her laughter at the filly's impatient prancing. "Walk, Gypsy," she repeated firmly and was pleased to be obeyed.

"I think she could do it without the line," Wendy said as the filly circled her at a walk, a trot, and a canter, halting and reversing directions on command.

"She's a quick one," Uncle Art agreed. "Almost too quick. A smart horse is nearly as hard to train as a slower one. You always have to stay one step ahead of the smart ones."

"Whoa, Gypsy," Wendy ordered, then called the filly in, petting her for a moment before she unhooked the line from her halter. "Go play," she said, laughing as the filly went streaking off, bucking and shying at her own shadow as she raced it across the grass.

The rest of the training session was more serious as Wendy worked with all the other yearlings. They were catching on and fairly obedient to her commands, though one young colt couldn't seem to control his excited bucks when she ordered him to canter, and a timid filly insisted on coming in to her every time she was told to whoa.

19

By the time Gypsy and the rest of them were back in the corral, Wendy's shoulders and arms ached, and she was dizzy from going around in circles.

"Think they'll ever catch on?" Wendy asked as she helped Uncle Art unfasten the cinch of the bitting rig that he'd been using on a two-year-old colt.

"They're just like little kids," he said. "They don't concentrate very well now, and they'll forget most of it when we turn them out with the other horses, but when we work them again in the fall, it'll come back. The more a horse is worked and handled when he's young, the easier he is to train when he gets older."

"Maybe I should have started riding earlier," Wendy said with a giggle.

Though she'd ridden her uncle's prize stallion, Happy Warrior, on the rescue mission that had made Gypsy her horse, Wendy hadn't done any riding in the two weeks since. Now the Saddle Club ride loomed ahead, and her feeling of inadequacy was coming back. It was one thing to work with Gypsy and the other yearlings, since they couldn't be ridden, but to take the responsibility for another horse, one that could make mistakes. . . .

"Are you going to bring in Nimblefoot?" Wendy asked without thinking.

"Nimblefoot?" For a moment her uncle looked puzzled, then asked, "The gelding that the Webster boy was so crazy about?"

Wendy nodded. "Aunt Laura was talking about him today. She told me what happened."

"It was too bad," her uncle said, "both because of the injury to the horse and because it happened so late in their stay. I think I might have been able to get Jimmy to riding again if they hadn't left so soon."

"Was he afraid to ride?" Wendy asked.

"More or less." Her uncle picked up the training equipment and headed for the barn.

"What do you mean?" Wendy asked, following him.

"He blamed Nimblefoot for what happened . . . said the horse tried to buck on the trail."

"Did he?" Wendy was shocked.

Uncle Art shrugged. "It's hard to tell what happened. Things like that happen so quickly, and

21

Jimmy might not have been able to tell a buck from a stumble."

"How is the horse? I mean, is he all right now?"

Her uncle turned to look at her, and Wendy could sense the speculation in his gaze. "How would you like to find out for us?" he asked.

"How?" she asked hesitantly.

"Well, we're going after some of the dude horses this afternoon, so why don't we bring Nimblefoot in, too? You could ride him around a little and see how he acts. Dr. James was pretty sure that the shoulder would heal cleanly, but there's no way to be sure except by riding him."

"What could be wrong with it?"

"It could have left him weak or stiff on that side, and if he is, I want to know about it right away. I don't want any inexperienced riders on an unsafe horse."

Wendy started to open her mouth to protest that she wasn't exactly an experienced rider, but before she could speak, they were interrupted by the sound of horses approaching. Cliff Harris and George Trent, the two ranch hands, rode up.

"Find anything interesting?" Uncle Art asked

as the men—Cliff short, stocky, and redheaded; George tall, dark, lean, and Indian-looking—dismounted.

George shook his head. "Fences are fine, and the cattle look good. I don't think we lost a single calf in the blizzard."

"That's good news." Uncle Art smiled. "Just put your horses in stalls for now. We'll be going after the dude horses as soon as we finish lunch."

"Think you'll get the Webster kid back on a horse?" Cliff asked before leading his horse into the barn.

"We'll all have to try," Uncle Art said. "Maybe if he sees Wendy riding the pinto. . . ." His eyes were speculative. "After all, he's only a couple of years younger than Wendy, so he should feel a challenge to try again himself."

"I'd sure like to know if the horse did buck on the trail," George said as the two men disappeared into the barn.

Wendy said nothing as she walked beside her uncle, but she was beginning to feel an uncomfortable similarity between Jimmy Webster's problems and her own.

2 · Wendy Meets Nimblefoot

You want to go out and help us pick a mount for you, Wendy?" Uncle Art asked when they finished lunch.

Wendy considered for a moment, then shook her head. "I don't know any of the horses," she said. "You can pick out the right one for me better than I could."

"Most of the dude horses are gentle enough, but you'll want one with spirit, too—a horse that's fun to ride," Uncle Art said.

Cliff and George nodded their agreement, but Wendy didn't say anything. Somehow, she didn't share their confidence in her ability to take care of a horse while riding it.

"Maybe you should take the time to finish your

red blouse," Aunt Laura suggested. "Summer sewing time is hard to come by, and you did say you wanted to wear it on the ride tomorrow."

Wendy laughed. "I thought I'd have a lot more time once I finished studying and took the tests Mrs. Carter gave me, but this last week has gone so fast. I'll probably forget how to sew and knit by fall."

"You can't give up knitting till you get my slippers done," Uncle Art reminded her. "I can't be running around with holes in my slippers all summer."

"I'm still not sure you'll want to wear the ones I'm knitting," Wendy said with a giggle. "I keep making mistakes."

"You're doing fine," her aunt assured her. "Let's get the dishes into the dishwasher. Then I'll help you put the collar on your blouse."

They worked together so easily and efficiently that Wendy had a hard time believing she'd only lived on the Cross R Ranch for two months. In some ways, life with her father in Phoenix after her mother died seemed to have happened to someone else, and she felt at home here. Still, there were problems here, too—problems that involved horses and riding.

Wendy swallowed a sigh as she followed her aunt through the swinging doors from the kitchen, through the dining room, and into the hall that led past her bedroom, the guest bath, and her aunt and uncle's room. Only when they were in the cluttered sewing room could she push aside her nibbling worries enough to settle down to work on the red print blouse.

"Are you worried about the ride?" Aunt Laura asked as Wendy snipped the threads between the buttonholes and then settled the nearly finished blouse on the ironing board to mark the places where she would be sewing on the buttons.

"A little," Wendy admitted. "I've never been on a trail ride before. At the riding stable there were several large pastures where we could ride around, but they didn't like to let people take the horses out away from the stable grounds." She swallowed hard. "They were right, weren't they?"

"You have to stop feeling guilty about what happened to Buck, Wendy," her aunt said. "I've told you before—accidents happen. Horses fall or run away, or they can get hurt just running around the pasture. Remember, if it hadn't been for you, Gypsy would have died in the barbed wire and Mr. Benson would have lost his mare and foal in the blizzard."

"I know, but—" Before she could go on, Gypsy's shrill whinny, echoed by all the horses in the small corral, interrupted them.

"They must be coming with the horses," Aunt Laura said, setting down the bright-printed peasant dress she'd been hemming. "Shall we go watch them?"

Wendy followed her aunt, with a mixture of apprehension and excitement. Having Gypsy for her very own horse was the most important thing that had ever happened to her, but the Morgan filly was only a yearling, so she couldn't be ridden at all for at least a year, and even then only gently and carefully. Until Gypsy was older, Wendy would have to ride other horses, and that, she knew, wasn't going to be easy.

By the time they reached the area of the big corral, the small herd of horses was already trotting across the high grass of the home pasture, followed by the three mounted men. Wendy watched the horses closely, wondering which one was Nimblefoot. As soon as they were inside the big corral, she hurried to close the double gates, fastening the new Gypsy-proof latch carefully.

"What do you think, Wendy?" Uncle Art asked as he slipped off Happy Warrior, his big Appaloosa stallion, and came over to lean on the fence with Wendy and her aunt. "Which ones do you want to try?"

Wendy felt his eyes but didn't look around, preferring to study the eight horses that were milling around the corral. "Which one is Nimblefoot?" she asked at last.

"The black and white pinto on the far side," her uncle answered. "We called him Nimblefoot because he was always bouncing ahead on the rides. Went anywhere, like a mountain goat."

"He looks a lot like Carol's Quito," Wendy said, thinking about the girl on the next ranch, who had, in the two weeks since their terrible experience in the blizzard, become her best friend. "Except that Quito's brown and white, of course."

"Does he seem sound?" Aunt Laura asked.

"Without having ridden him, he does," Uncle Art said. "Want to try him, Wendy?" He stepped away from the fence and started to get his rope off his saddle.

"I'll try any of them that you think would be right," Wendy said, fighting a cold feeling in the pit of her stomach. "Which other ones would be good?"

Uncle Art studied the horses. "The little bay is good, and so is the buckskin over near the gate. The sorrel mare would be fine, and so would the black. He's a little older, but he's a good mountain or trail horse."

"I see you brought in Ladybug," Wendy said, reaching out to pat the graying muzzle of the old dun mare, and remembering painfully that she'd even been afraid to ride this gentle, willing horse.

"I thought maybe we could get Jimmy started riding again on her. I mean, if he's changed his mind about blaming all horses for Nimblefoot's fall." Uncle Art didn't sound too hopeful.

"You don't think he'll want Nimblefoot?" Wendy asked, her eyes straying to where the black and white horse was trading friendly sniffs over the fence with Gypsy.

"Not unless he's changed a lot," Uncle Art said. "Anyway, if I can get him on a horse again, it will be an experienced one like the black, at least until I'm convinced that he knows what he's doing."

"Maybe I should start out the same way," Wendy suggested, the sinking feeling growing instead of shrinking as the conversation went on.

"Oh, no, you're something else," her uncle said, one hand warm on her shoulder. "You always think of the horse first, like a real horseman. That's more important than experience. You'll learn the rest of it, and I know you'll take care of the horse you're riding while you're learning."

Wendy swallowed hard, then forced a smile. "I hope you're right," she said, without too much confidence. Though she loved horses, she couldn't forget that her carelessness in Phoenix had allowed Buck to shy into the path of the pickup truck, costing him his life.

"Want to start with the little bay?" Uncle Art asked, picking up his rope and going into the corral with the horses. It took him only a moment to slip the rope over the bay's head and lead him

30

out of the corral to where George and Cliff were waiting with a bridle and the saddle Wendy had been using.

The horse was quickly saddled, and Wendy was very much aware of all the eyes watching her as she gathered the reins and turned the stirrup forward for mounting. Nervousness was a heavy weight in her stomach as she swung aboard. The bay bounced a little, then settled down without an argument, responding to her touch as a well-trained horse should.

The next three horses were less difficult to mount and ride around the grassy area, and Wendy felt the knot of fear easing a little with each trial. Still, she felt nothing special for any of the horses. They were good horses, well trained and pleasant to ride, but none of them touched off the special warmth that she'd felt the moment she first saw the half-wild Gypsy.

"Still feel like giving Nimblefoot a try?" her uncle asked. "Or did one of the others suit you?"

"I'll try him," Wendy said. "You want to know about his shoulder, anyway, don't you?"

The young gelding was quickly caught and

31

saddled, but Wendy didn't mount right away, pausing instead to pet him and talk to him. His shoulder showed the marks of his fall, in ridged lines that disturbed the smoothness of his muscles.

"He needs a good brushing," Wendy observed, scrubbing lightly at the patches of winter hair that clung here and there. "In fact, they all do."

"Can't expect them to be all shed out," George said. "It's only been two weeks since they needed their winter hair to keep warm."

"He's a pretty horse," Wendy said, moving around to the saddle. "How old is he?"

"Around five, I think," Uncle Art said, then added, "Shorten up your reins a little, honey; he just might be feeling good enough to buck. He hasn't been ridden for close to a year, you know."

Wendy did as she was told, but the little pinto merely danced sideways as she settled into the saddle. "It's all right, boy," she said, loosening the reins a little and petting first one shoulder, then the other. "You just need to get some of the pasture kinks out, don't you?"

"Start out easy," her uncle counseled. "Walk him in figure eights, then trot. See if he shows

32

any hesitation in turning with that shoulder."

Nimblefoot danced along, not hard to hold but so eager to please that she longed to let him go. He moved smoothly from walk to trot and then bounced gaily into a lope, showing no sign of weakness or hesitation.

"Looks like he's healed fine, just like the vet said," Cliff observed.

"How does he feel?" Aunt Laura asked as Wendy started the gelding in another figure eight, this time at a little faster lope.

"He's a—" Wendy began, but before she could go any further, she was interrupted by a loud whinny from the smaller corral, where Gypsy and the other young horses had been watching the proceedings over the fence. Now, however, Gypsy was staring the other way and whinnying more greetings. In a moment two riders came cantering up.

Wendy recognized Carol on the small brown and white pinto, and a second later realized that the redheaded young man on the tall bay was Kirk Donahue, nephew of the veterinarian, Dr. James. She reined Nimblefoot around and rode over to say hello to them.

"Isn't that the little gelding that was hurt last summer?" Kirk asked as soon as they'd exchanged greetings.

"Nimblefoot?" Carol said, proving that Aunt Laura had been right when she told Wendy that their nearest neighbor knew practically every horse in the state.

Wendy nodded. "Uncle Art wanted me to try riding him to see if he's sound."

"Is he?" Kirk asked, dismounting from his bay and dropping the reins. "Have you checked him out? His shoulder was an awful mess. Everybody but Uncle Hal thought it was broken. They were ready to destroy him."

"I'm glad they didn't," Wendy said, sliding down to stroke the black and white shoulder. "He's a darling horse."

"Are you going to ride him tomorrow?" Carol asked, inspecting the healed shoulder along with Kirk.

Wendy hesitated for a moment, then left them to let Gypsy out of the corral before answering. The little filly raced over to where the three horses

34

were standing and paused to sniff noses with them. Then she greeted Kirk and Carol with an enthusiasm that proved her bad experience with the horse thief was now forgotten.

"What about it?" Aunt Laura asked as she and Uncle Art joined the group.

Wendy felt all eyes turned in her direction, but the ones that touched her most were the brown, intelligent ones that Nimblefoot fastened on her. There was almost a look of pleading in the horse's gaze, as though he really wanted to be her horse for the summer. It was Gypsy, however, who took the lead, quite literally.

Catching the pinto's trailing reins in her teeth, the graceful Morgan filly walked over to Wendy, Nimblefoot right behind her. "Do I have a choice?" Wendy asked through her laughter as the two horses both nuzzled her, sniffing at the scent of horse cubes that never seemed absent from the pockets of her jeans and shirts.

3 · Ghost Story

ARE YOU SURE you want to let those two make up your mind for you?" Aunt Laura asked, pointing to the dainty filly and the larger, sturdier gelding.

"They just confirmed my opinion," Wendy said. "I really like Nimblefoot, and I think he likes me, too."

"You'll have to be a little more cautious with him than you would be with another horse," Uncle Art warned. "After what happened with Jimmy. . . ." His voice trailed off. "I just want you to be careful."

"I will," Wendy said, putting one arm over the neck of each horse. "With all this moral support, I can hardly miss."

"Gypsy may be around to help here," Aunt

Laura said, "but she's not going to be able to go with you all the time, you know."

"That's what we came over to talk about," Carol said. "Gypsy, I mean."

"What about her?" Wendy asked.

"We had an after-school meeting about her," Kirk said, grinning. "This was our last day, you know."

"We voted and elected Gypsy mascot of the Junior Saddle Club," Carol said, looking pleased.

"Sounds very impressive," Aunt Laura said before Wendy could speak, "but what does it mean?"

"That Gypsy will be welcome to come on the rides with us, even though she's too young to be ridden," Kirk said happily. Then he grinned at Wendy. "It was Carol's idea," he added, "but we all thought you'd like coming better if you could have her with you."

"I . . . I don't know what to say." Wendy gulped, having a hard time speaking around the lump that seemed to have formed in her throat. Tears burned slightly in her eyes.

"Before you say anything besides thank you, I

37

think you ought to see how that little filly will act on a ride with other horses," Uncle Art suggested, a warning note in his voice. "A loose horse can be trouble, you know, especially in a big group of horses."

"Oh," Wendy said, her happiness fading, "I hadn't thought of that."

"Why don't you give her a trial ride?" Aunt Laura suggested. "You could go somewhere around here and see how she behaves herself."

"How about going now?" Carol said. "It would give you a chance to get better acquainted with Nimblefoot, too."

"Sounds like a good idea to me," Kirk said. "What about it?"

Wendy looked from her uncle to her aunt. "Would it be all right?" she asked.

"I don't see why not," Uncle Art said. "It'll give you a chance to see whether or not you'll need to keep her on a lead rope."

"The way those two horses hit it off, I don't think it'll be much of a problem," Kirk said as he mounted the bay, Apache. Gypsy and Nimblefoot were, indeed, standing with their noses together,

looking rather like a pair of conspirators planning their next move.

Wendy mounted the gelding with only a twinge of nervousness. "Come on, Gypsy," she said as she reined the pinto alongside Quito and Carol.

"Maybe you can teach her to heel like a dog," Carol suggested with a giggle.

They rode around the home pasture for a while, then slowed their pace as they neared the gate to the lake pasture. Gypsy, who had always followed Wendy like a dog when she was hiking, seemed to find the addition of Nimblefoot perfectly all right. She stayed at the pinto's side as though held by a rope, suiting her pace to his and venturing no more than a dozen feet in either direction.

"That is truly wild," Carol said. "I've seen little foals that wandered farther than that from their mothers. She's really good."

"She's used to staying with me," Wendy said. Then she asked, "Where are we going?"

"How about Gulligan Gulch?" Kirk suggested.

"Where's that?" Wendy asked.

"It's in your uncle's north pasture," Carol answered. "It's kind of rough country, so you can see what kind of trail horse Nimblefoot is."

"It'll be a good test for Gypsy," Kirk added. "Okay?"

"You know the ranch better than I do," Wendy said, "but aren't we headed wrong for the north pasture? I thought the gate to it was on the other side of Happy's private paddock."

"It is," Carol agreed. "We can come back that way, but since we're this close, why don't we ride to the lake pasture and check the horses? We can cut across and use the old gate between the two pastures, then come back by Gulligan Gulch. It's really not too far from your house, you know."

"No, I didn't," Wendy admitted. "In fact, I've never heard of it before. What is it, exactly?"

"It's a deep cut in the hills, kind of like a shallow box canyon, with a spring at one end and a little stream running along the bottom," Kirk supplied.

"So how'd it get the name?" Wendy asked, pleased at the way Nimblefoot moved right up to the gate and stood while she leaned down to unfasten it. He backed and pivoted to let the others through first, then moved into position again so that she could refasten the latch without dismounting.

"I'll be glad when I get Quito well enough trained for maneuvers like that," Carol said with a sigh.

"I think you're doing real well," Kirk said. "You've only been working with him for about six weeks, haven't you?"

Carol nodded. "I guess I do expect too much," she admitted. "Now that school is out, though, he's going to be getting a lot more work, so he should progress faster."

The horse talk continued till they finished surveying the horse herd and passed judgment on the five Appaloosa foals that stood with their mothers in the big pasture they shared with the dude horses. Only as they left the meadow, and moved into the trees that grew between the meadow and the hilly north pasture, did Wendy remember her earlier question.

"What about the gulch?" she asked. "Where did it get that name? Did someone named Gulligan own this ranch before Uncle Art?"

"No, it was named long before there was a

ranch here," Kirk said. "About a hundred years ago, when this area was just being settled, an old man who was a trapper and prospector built a cabin at the end of the gulch. His name was Gulligan."

Wendy waited for him to go on, but they rode in silence for several minutes. Finally, sensing that there must be more to the story, she asked, "Is that all? How come they named it for him?"

Carol sighed. "He's supposed to haunt the gulch. At least, that's the story I've heard. I don't know if it's true or not. I mean, about what happened to him."

"What did happen to him?" Wendy asked.

"He was a real hermit," Kirk said. "Just went into town when he had to. Traded his furs for supplies, then disappeared again for months at a time. The last time he went into town, there was a killing and a robbery. Everyone blamed the old man for it, so they formed a vigilante group and rode out to his cabin."

"What did the vigilantes do to the man in the gulch?" Wendy asked when he seemed to hesitate.

"That's where the stories get vague," Kirk said.

"I've heard about four versions—everything from asking him to leave, to riding him out on a rail, to hanging him from his own cabin ridgepole."

"Is that why he's supposed to haunt the gulch?" Wendy asked, shivering slightly at the thought that such a thing could have happened so near the ranch house.

Kirk nodded. "When you see the place, you'll understand. It's pretty weird down there. I don't know how anyone could stand to live in such a place . . . especially alone."

"I'm dying to see it," Wendy said.

"I suppose we'd better get moving if we want to have time to explore the gulch," Carol said. "I'm not exactly sure where the gate is."

Wendy laughed. "By all means, let's hurry," she said. "I'm anxious to meet the ghost."

"No ghost in the daytime," Kirk said. "If you want to see him, we'll have to make a night visit, as Dan and Evan Raither did."

"You mean someone has actually seen the ghost?" Wendy asked with amusement.

"That's what they said," Kirk answered, chuckling. "Of course, that was a couple of years ago,

44

but I don't think anyone has tried to spend the night in the cabin since."

Wendy shook her head in amazement. It seemed strange that her aunt and uncle had never mentioned the gulch, with its colorful history. It made such a good story and. . . . Her speculation was ended as Carol announced that she'd spotted the gate to the north pasture.

Once they passed through the gate, Wendy began to feel a change in Nimblefoot. He seemed to be lagging behind a little, hesitating as the land got rougher.

Could he be tired? she asked herself. They hadn't been riding hard, but perhaps, after the long days in the pasture. . . . She clung to that thought with increasing worry, until Carol said that they were almost to their destination.

"We should reach the gulch trail just beyond that little grove of pines," Kirk said, urging Apache into a lope. "We've been riding parallel to the gulch for a while now."

Wendy loped after him, rushing Nimblefoot in her eagerness. She was just opening her mouth to speak, when Nimblefoot skidded to a stop and

45

began to shake. She touched him with her heel, not sure what had frightened him. However, he refused to move more than a few feet beyond the trees.

Kirk and Apache, who had been in the lead, were already on the cliff trail, but Carol turned Quito back. "What is it?" she asked.

Wendy turned the gelding in a circle, then tried to force him forward, but he only shook harder, stumbling over his own hooves as he tried to turn away. "He acts scared to death," Wendy said. "Do you think this could be where it happened?"

"I doubt it," Carol said. "Not if it was a dude ride. But there are places like this all over the area, and it was a rocky trail, I know."

"What'll I do with him?" Wendy asked, realizing that urging him forward was getting her nowhere.

"We could try leading him," Kirk said, riding back, "but I don't think it would be smart to drag him along that narrow trail."

"Oh, no, he'd fall for sure," Wendy said quickly.

"We could ride back to the far end and go in that way," Carol said. "It's a lot farther, but it is passable along the bottom of the gulch.''

"It's getting too late," Kirk said, shaking his head. "If we want to explore the cabin, we have to get down there before the shadows are too long."

"Let's leave the horses here, then," Carol suggested. "It's not far to walk, and they can graze a little. Maybe it will help Nimblefoot if he can just stand here, without any pressure to go down on the trail."

She didn't sound too confident of that idea, but Wendy was in no mood to argue, for some of the gelding's terror had communicated itself to her, and her own knees felt a little weak as she slid down. In some ways, she almost wished that she could stay here with Gypsy and Nimblefoot and let the others explore the haunted gulch.

4 · Gulligan Gulch

THE TRAIL wasn't really a difficult one after they passed the first narrow area, yet Wendy found herself looking around apprehensively at the solid rock wall that rose on one side and the sheer drop to the gloomy canyon floor on the other. It wasn't hard to imagine what it had been like the night the vigilantes came and—

Wendy stopped, suddenly curious about the story. "What about Gulligan?" she asked. "Did he really kill the person in town?"

"I think that's what started the ghost stories," Kirk said. "About a week after the vigilantes came up here, they found the real murderer."

"So they killed an innocent man," Wendy said with a shiver.

48

"If they did kill him," Carol said calmly. "The whole story could just be a legend, you know. I heard one version that claimed old Gulligan held the vigilantes captive on this trail for two days."

"What?" Kirk stopped and looked around. "Where'd you hear that?"

Carol shrugged. "I don't remember. I just know that whoever it was said that Gulligan climbed up on the other side of the gulch and sat behind a rock or something. He got the vigilantes between two exposed points on the trail, and every time one of them tried to go either up or down, he'd shoot at him."

Wendy laughed, liking that version better than the others.

"Hey, you can see the cabin from here," Kirk called, moving ahead, and in a moment, Wendy could see the rest of Gulligan Gulch. It was a miniature box canyon, not very wide, with a small stream that ran from the cabin down through the gulch. Thick grass covered the ground, and there were a number of small trees and bushes partially hiding the tumbledown cabin that nestled under the overhanging rocks at the end of the gulch.

"Do you think we should explore it?" Carol asked, hesitating a little now that they'd reached the floor of the gulch.

"Sure, come on." Kirk went striding across the turf, without any sign of caution, and Wendy followed him as quickly as she could, though she couldn't shake the feeling that someone or *something* was watching them.

"I don't see how anyone could stay down here at night," Carol said, making it clear that she shared Wendy's feelings about the spooky gulch. "Old Gulligan must have been crazy."

"He built a sturdy cabin, anyway," Kirk said, opening the weathered old door with hardly a squeak. "This place has stood here through a lot of hard winters."

The single room was bare-looking, in spite of the rough wooden table and two chairs that stood against one wall. Dim light entered from the small single window in the same wall as the door. Wendy moved across the creaking wood floor cautiously, expecting it to give way beneath her at any moment.

"Where does that go?" Carol asked, pointing

into the shadows at the rear of the room.

By straining her eyes, Wendy could see that there was a door in the rear wall of the cabin, but she didn't hurry toward it. Instead, her attention was drawn to the table. Curious, she reached out to rub its surface. The wood was surprisingly clear of dust and dirt, though the floor of the room was thick with gritty dust.

"Want to find out?" Kirk asked Carol as the two of them stood close to the rear door. His grin was wicked as he added, "Maybe that's where the ghost of old Gulligan hides during the day."

"Oh, come on," Carol protested, her tone only slightly betraying her doubts. "It probably just opens into some sort of storage area."

Wendy joined them, not because she particularly cared what lay behind the door, but because the clean tabletop seemed strangely sinister in the deserted building. Kirk was trying the door, twisting the knob and tugging. "Is it locked?" Wendy asked, almost hopefully.

"Just . . . uh . . . stuck, I think." Kirk gave the door a mighty kick, then jerked it again. It swung open with a screech of protest, showing nothing

51

but blackness beyond. The dank, unpleasant odor of damp earth filled the room.

"Hey, do you suppose this is an escape tunnel?" Kirk asked, stepping gingerly into the darkness.

"I don't see any light at the end," Carol said doubtfully.

"I wish we had some matches or a candle or something," Kirk said. "I'd like to explore this." He took another step, then stopped and bent down. "There's something in here."

"What is it?" Wendy asked, her mind supplying a few gruesome possibilities that she quickly dismissed as the result of too much TV watching —dead bodies had no place on a Montana dude ranch, she was sure.

"Just some old burlap bags," Kirk said disappointedly as he dragged one of them far enough into the cabin to see it.

"I'll bet Gulligan used this as a sort of root cellar," Carol said. "He didn't go into town for supplies very often, so he'd have to keep them stored somewhere, and this place would be cool even in the summer."

Kirk sighed. "I guess you're right," he said,

backing out and closing the door behind him, "but I'd still like to get a light and explore that cave, or whatever it is, sometime."

Carol nodded, then looked at her watch. "Not today," she said. "Do you realize it's nearly four already? I promised Mom I'd be home by five, and we've still got to walk out of here."

Wendy gladly turned away from the door in the back wall, but not before she realized that there was something odd about the sack Kirk had dragged out of the cave. She followed him and Carol slowly, trying to puzzle out what it was. She was almost to the bushes that concealed the beginning of the ridge trail before she realized the truth: The sack had looked fine—like any other burlap bag—only it was supposed to be a hundred years old!

Wendy started forward, hurrying to catch Kirk and Carol and ask them if they could explain it. However, before she could take more than a couple of strides, there was a stirring in the bushes. Kirk and Carol stopped, too, and they all turned toward the sound. Wendy tensed, ready to run, though she had no idea what she expected to see.

53

A slender sorrel head emerged over the top of a thick growth of wild roses, and Gypsy's whicker protested the fact that she couldn't get through the thorny wall. Relief sent them all into gales of laughter, while Gypsy's one blue eye and one brown eye turned, with curiosity, from one person to another.

"You nearly scared us to death, Gypsy," Wendy gasped between peals of laughter. "We thought you were the ghost."

Gypsy, apparently disgusted, disappeared back into the trees, then came bouncing around the end of the little pine grove. She nuzzled Wendy eagerly and was rewarded with a rather battered horse cube.

"She must have gotten bored and followed us down," Kirk said, looking embarrassed at his own frightened reaction.

"Trust her not to stay with the horses," Wendy agreed. "I think she figures she's a person."

"She almost is," Carol said, reaching out to rub the filly's neck and scratch behind her ears. "At least, she's more like a dog than a horse."

"Well, we'd better get up there and see what

54

the others are doing." Kirk headed for the beginning of the trail.

"I hope Nimblefoot hasn't wandered off," Wendy said, her mind returning abruptly to the unhappy pinto.

"What are you going to do with him?" Carol asked as they started along the rocky trail.

Wendy sighed. "I wish I knew," she said. "He's a good horse, and I really like riding him, but if he gets that scared of a trail, I just don't know how to help him."

"Maybe he'll get over it," Kirk suggested. "After all, he hasn't been ridden at all since his fall—till today, I mean—so maybe he just needs a chance to regain his confidence. Once he finds out that he won't fall on a narrow trail. . . ."

"Do you really think he will get over it?" Wendy asked when Kirk's words trailed off. "Do you think he'll be all right for the ride tomorrow?"

Kirk didn't answer for a moment, and then he turned to Carol. "We're riding to Bay Meadows for the steak fry, aren't we?" he asked.

She nodded.

Again Kirk seemed to consider. He said,

"There's some rough country on the ride out, but no cliffs or ridge trails like the one into the gulch —nothing worse than what we came over today."

"He was acting funny before we got to the trail," Wendy said slowly, suddenly wondering if Nimblefoot had been nervous instead of tired.

"Maybe he'll feel better around more horses," Carol suggested. "I've known trail horses that were fine in a big bunch and kind of strange when you rode them alone."

"He was with Quito and Apache and Gypsy today," Wendy reminded them.

"Maybe you should keep riding him around here for while," Kirk said. "Give him a little more time to get adjusted to it."

Wendy thought about it all the rest of the way up the steep trail, weighing her desire to help the gelding against her fear that she might make a mistake and hurt him even more. By the time they reached the horses, she still wasn't sure of anything, except the fact that she cared very much what happened to Nimblefoot. She spent a few minutes petting him and talking to him before she mounted and tried, slowly and carefully, to

57

turn him toward the gulch.

For a moment, he seemed rooted to the ground, but then he took one hesitant step toward the beginning of the trail. Wendy urged him again, talking as soothingly as she could. He took another step, then stumbled, his whole body shaking with fear. Tears burned her eyes as she forced him to stand for a few minutes before allowing him to turn and follow the other horses. Even before she leaned forward to pat his shoulder, she knew it would be wet with the sweat of his terrible fear.

Still, the rest of the ride seemed to go better, though the country didn't improve much until they neared the ranch house. Nimblefoot lagged a little and stumbled twice; but by the time they reached the gate, which opened not too far from Happy's paddock, Wendy was beginning to hope that she might be able to help Nimblefoot regain his confidence.

"I know what it's like to be afraid, Nimblefoot," she whispered to him as she stroked his neck, "but I know you can get over it if you'll just try."

"We'd better be riding on," Kirk said as he closed the gate behind Gypsy. "We'll see you tomorrow, for the steak fry."

"Sure, see you." Wendy waved, but her thoughts were already centered on the figure that had emerged from the barn. Her Uncle Art was waiting, and she knew that he would have a lot of questions to ask about Nimblefoot—questions she might find hard to answer.

5 · Trouble on the Trail

WELL, HOW did it go?" Uncle Art asked as soon as she reached the barn.

"He's a darling horse," Wendy said, knowing that she was evading the question. "I just love him."

"I'm glad to hear that. I was pretty worried."

Wendy swallowed a twinge of guilt. "Oh, why?" she asked. "Did you think he'd do something bad?"

"Not bad, really. Dangerous. His injury seems fine, but a serious fall like that can leave a weakness that only shows up later, when he's tired or upset." His eyes narrowed. "Nothing like that happened, did it?"

"Not a weakness," Wendy said, hating herself

for hedging. "He did get real nervous when we rode into a rocky area. In fact, he refused to go along the trail, but I suppose that might be because it looked like the place where he fell."

Her uncle nodded, but he looked worried. "You think he remembers his fall?" he asked.

"He was scared enough to be shaking."

"That doesn't sound good."

"I think he'll get over it," she said with what she hoped sounded like more confidence than she felt. "I mean, I know what it is to be afraid to do something, and I'll work with him, Uncle Art. He just needs to get his self-confidence back. Once he realizes that he won't fall, just because he's on a narrow trail. . . ." She let it fade, not liking the look on her uncle's face.

"I don't know, Wendy," he said.

"I'll be careful."

"I know you will, and I know you're a good rider and a good horseman, but that might not be enough."

"What do you mean?" Wendy felt suddenly cold.

"You overcame your fear of riding because you

61

loved Gypsy enough to ride another horse to save her, but Nimblefoot. . . . A horse like that is a danger, honey, to himself and to anyone who rides him. I almost wish that I hadn't listened to Dr. James. It would have been easier to destroy him then."

"Destroy him?" Wendy could hardly say the words. "You can't!"

"I can't keep a dangerous horse on this ranch, honey."

"You could sell him."

"And have him panic and kill someone? I couldn't do that."

"Maybe we could tell them not to ride him on mountain trails or. . . ." Wendy felt panic of her own as she listened to her uncle. "Uncle Art, you can't just kill a horse because he's afraid."

"I don't want to," he said, and his troubled eyes told her that he meant it. "He's a nice little horse. I know, because I did most of his training myself, but—"

"Won't you give him a chance? This is the first time he's been ridden, and he didn't do anything wrong. I mean—" She gulped, tears clogging her

62

throat. "Maybe it was me. Maybe I upset him and. . . ."

"Hey, take it easy now," said Uncle Art, his hand warm on her shoulder. "I'm not going to do anything with him right now. I just wanted you to know—to realize—that it's an eventuality that might have to be faced, Wendy. I thought the sooner you realized it, the better."

"You will give him another chance, won't you? You'll let me ride him and try to help him?" Wendy's words tumbled out on a tide of fear.

"Tomorrow?"

"Sure." Wendy spoke quickly, trying to sound confident. "I know he'll do fine."

"I wish I were going along."

"Aren't you?" Wendy was surprised.

"I gave George and Cliff the weekend off, so one of us has to stay here in case the Websters come early. Laura signed up to help fry the steaks, so I'm elected to run the ranch." His face didn't reflect his casual tone. "I'd feel better if you rode a different horse."

"Nimblefoot needs to be ridden," Wendy said. "He has to learn to love and trust me if I'm going to help him get over his problems."

Her uncle shrugged. "Well, put him and Gypsy in stalls for tonight. I've already fed the other horses, so they'll have to eat in here."

"Right away," Wendy said, hoping as she did so that she knew what she was doing. She was desperately afraid of the trial she was subjecting Nimblefoot to, yet she was equally afraid to leave him home where Uncle Art might decide to test the horse himself.

Such thoughts haunted her through the evening as she hemmed her red blouse, sewed the buttons on, and pressed it to wear on the ride. As she opened the window by her bed so that Abigail the cat could come and go throughout the night, she couldn't help looking at the cloudless sky and wishing for rain.

The morning, however, dawned bright and clear, a perfect day for a ride. All too soon, Wendy and her aunt were saddling Nimblefoot and the sorrel mare that had been brought in with the rest of the dude horses. "Where do we go?" Wendy asked as she allowed Gypsy to lead Nimblefoot out of the barn.

"To the Carter place to meet Carol and her mother, and probably Kirk, then on around the lakeshore to the Bay Meadows trail. The club is supposed to meet there."

"Is it far beyond the Carters?"

"Not very. We have plenty of time. Why?"

"No reason. I was just curious about how long a ride it would be."

"The Bay Meadows trail isn't very long, and we'll come back through some public grazing land, so the whole ride won't be more than an hour and a half or two hours each way." They rode in silence for a moment, then Aunt Laura asked, "Are you worrying about Nimblefoot? Art told me that he was concerned about him."

"I just don't want to be too hard on him right away," Wendy said. "I want to give him a real chance, Aunt Laura. It takes time to learn not to be afraid, and I want Nimblefoot to have time."

"So do we, Wendy," her aunt said. "We just don't want to buy that time at the cost of having you hurt. Okay?"

The trip to the Carters' proved easy enough, and both Gypsy and Nimblefoot were on their

65

best behavior. Peg Carter, now looking more like her daughter Carol and less like a teacher, greeted them happily, though she was already murmuring doubts about the wisdom of starting her summer's riding with a trail ride.

"I may be eating off the mantel for a week," she said, and Carol giggled.

Wendy had only a few minutes to tell Carol and Kirk about her uncle's fears that he might have to have Nimblefoot destroyed, before they were joined by other riders from the surrounding ranches. By the time they reached the area of the Bay Meadows trail, there were more than a dozen riders, and Wendy was busy talking and laughing with them.

At first, things went well on the ride. Nimblefoot proved once more that he was an excellent riding horse, and Gypsy stayed at his side obediently, snorting a little when the other riders crowded around but showing no sign of roaming. Before long, however, the crowd of riders had split into two separate groups, the youngsters going ahead of the older riders.

Wendy found herself the center of attention

and, though nervous, enjoyed it, since everyone seemed friendly and interested in knowing about the stray Morgan filly she'd rescued and finally purchased from her owner. It was some time before she felt the change in Nimblefoot. He stumbled twice, nearly pitching her out of the saddle, and when she touched his shoulders, she found that he was wet with nervous sweat.

Wendy looked up and saw the concern in Carol's face. "It's not much farther," she said softly, "but there is one ridge to cross before we drop down to Bay Springs, where they'll be cooking the food."

Wendy looked ahead and saw the raw, rocky hill and felt her own fears growing. "I don't think he'll make it," she confided to Carol. "I can feel him starting to shake already. It looks too much like the ridge near the gulch yesterday."

"If he stops here, your aunt will know there's something wrong," Carol said. "We've got to be smart and think of something."

"But what?" Wendy was close to tears at the thought that she might lose Nimblefoot because she'd chosen to ride him today.

"Give me Gypsy's lead," Carol said, riding Quito practically into Nimblefoot's nose.

Wendy handed it over, then swallowed hard as she saw that Carol had snapped it onto the rein ring of Nimblefoot's bridle. Carol wrapped it around her saddle horn several times, then looked at Wendy.

"Slap his rump as hard as you can," she said. "Try to get him running, and I'll do my best to keep him that way. If we can just get him to the top of the hill, so he can see that there's only meadow beyond, he should be all right."

Kirk, who'd ridden up on the other side, nodded. "I'll cut in right behind you," he said. "If we can keep him distracted, maybe he'll forget to be afraid." Then, much louder, he shouted, "Last one to the top of the hill has to string the rope corral."

The words worked like spurs on the other riders, and in a moment, Wendy felt that she'd been caught in a stampede. After three or four good slaps, Nimblefoot was at a dead run, and Carol's firm hold on the lead rope gave him no choice but to keep running. Gypsy bounded along at his side, delighted at the race, but Nimblefoot obviously didn't share her feeling.

Twice Wendy felt the little pinto begin to fight the rope, but each time, there was a snapping from behind and he went bounding ahead, stumbling a little but managing to stay on his feet. Somehow, they reached the crest of the hill, and Carol reined Quito in. Nimblefoot slid to a stop, shivering so hard that, for a moment, Wendy thought he might actually collapse.

"You okay?" Kirk asked, coiling his own rope back into place, then leaning down to smooth away the two marks he'd made when he slapped Nimblefoot with it.

Wendy drew a deep breath and lifted her reins as Carol unsnapped the lead. "I guess so," she said as the little gelding moved cautiously forward, his head down, "but look what it did to him. He was terrified, and we just made it worse."

Carol nodded sadly. "I'm sorry, Wendy, but I couldn't think of any other way to get him up that hill without letting your aunt see the way he acts. I mean, after what you told us. . . ."

Kirk sighed. "I know that's not the way to help

him, but what is? Your uncle might be right, Wendy. You can't just tell a horse that his fears are foolish and expect it to work. I'm not sure there *is* a way to help him."

"There has to be," Wendy said, one shaking hand rubbing the horse's sweat-slick shoulder while she clung to the saddle horn with the other. "Somehow, I've got to win his trust enough that he'll let me show him he doesn't have to be afraid."

"How?" Carol asked as they rode into the grove of trees, where the smoke of a dozen charcoal grills sweetened the noon breeze.

Wendy merely shook her head, wishing that she had an answer. Nimblefoot's very life depended on it.

6 · Jimmy

BY THE TIME the older riders reached them,
Wendy and the other young people had unsaddled their horses and turned them into the hastily
strung rope corral. Wendy hurried over to greet
her aunt and to offer to take care of the mare so
that Aunt Laura could go right to the grills and
help with the steak frying.

There was plenty going on in the grove, and
everyone seemed to be having a good time, but
Wendy couldn't be a part of it, no matter how
hard she tried. Her thoughts turned constantly to
Nimblefoot, and she hated herself for what she'd
allowed to happen. Instead of helping the horse
and gaining his trust, she'd been a part of forcing
him, of causing him more terror, of undoing what

little good yesterday's ride might have done.

While they ate the vast piles of potato salad, baked beans, and charcoal-broiled steaks, she confided her fears to Carol and Kirk. They both nodded in grim agreement. "It was a dumb thing to do," Kirk said, "but I kept thinking how it would look to your aunt if she saw him acting up the way he did yesterday."

"What am I going to do on the way home?" Wendy asked sorrowfully.

"Don't worry about it," Carol said. "The way back is all pasture and low hills—no rocky ridges at all."

Kirk nodded. "No one will notice a thing."

Wendy tried to smile at the reassurances, but her heart wasn't in it, for she realized that just hiding Nimblefoot's weakness from her aunt and uncle wasn't enough. If she couldn't cure the gelding's phobia about rocky ridges and narrow trails, he would be a constant source of danger to anyone who rode him.

Unable to talk about her fears, she gathered a handful of the carrot sticks left in one of the tubs of ice and carried them over to the rope barricade where Gypsy waited none too patiently. Nimblefoot, who'd been grazing a few feet away, came trotting up at once.

"I'm sorry, fella," Wendy said, breaking the sticks and feeding them to the two horses. "I didn't mean for you to be hurt and frightened again. I made a mistake, and I could have really hurt you by running you up that hill."

"Trouble?" The voice made her jump, and Wendy could feel the glow of guilt in her cheeks as she turned to face her aunt.

"Nimblefoot's not quite well, is he?" her aunt asked gently. "I saw him stumbling just before you all went racing up the hill together."

"He gets upset whenever we have to cross a rocky ridge," Wendy said.

"Are you sure it's just nerves, Wendy?"

"What do you mean?"

"A shoulder injury can be tricky. Art told you that. There's a possibility that he can't handle himself on rocky, uneven ground. His stumbling could be a sign of stiffness or pain from the way the muscles and tendons healed."

"But he's fine everywhere else," Wendy said.

"It's only when he hits a rocky ridge."

Aunt Laura shook her head. "He used to be like a mountain goat," she said sadly. "He'd climb anything."

"He will again," Wendy said, rubbing Nimblefoot's neck and trying to smooth the ridges of dried sweat away so that her aunt wouldn't see them. However, her aunt's hand followed hers, and Wendy could see the understanding in her face as she turned away from the horse.

"Wendy, I know that Art's promised to let you work with Nimblefoot for a little while, but you have to realize that not everything has a cure. There may be no way to help him, and I don't want you to find that out by getting hurt."

"I'll take it easy," Wendy said. "Just let me try."

Her aunt's expression was worried as she nodded. "We'll ride back together, all right?"

Wendy swallowed hard but offered no argument. She stayed with the two horses, Gypsy and Nimblefoot, while her aunt went back to help the other women put away the food and the men doused the fires and scraped the grills. In a few minutes, Carol and Kirk joined her.

74

"What happened?" Carol asked worriedly.

"She knew something was wrong. She's afraid that it might be more than just fear—that there may be something wrong with the way Nimblefoot's shoulder healed."

"What do you mean?" Kirk asked. "He's fine most of the time, isn't he?"

"Except on rocky ground," Wendy admitted. "I thought it was because the rough turf reminded him of where he fell, but Aunt Laura says it might be because the ground is uneven and causes his shoulder to hurt or something."

Carol looked as though she might argue the idea, but Kirk only frowned. "I'll ask Uncle Hal about that," he said. "He knows more about horses than anyone I've ever been around."

Carol nodded. "Other vets around the state are always calling Dr. James in for consultation when they get a real serious case."

"But what if it is something like that?" Wendy said. "Then there might be no help for him."

Nimblefoot, seeming to sense that Wendy was upset, rubbed his black and white nose against her, his dark eyes still trusting in spite of the rough way they'd all treated him on the hill. "It just can't be hopeless," Wendy said, fighting tears. "There has to be something we can do!"

Carol and Kirk stayed with her for a few minutes, but neither of them seemed to have much to offer in the way of comfort. It was almost a relief when they wandered off to help in cleaning up the picnic grounds.

It appeared that they would soon be riding home, and Wendy couldn't help being glad. In spite of the warm welcome she'd received from the young Saddle Club members, this had been far from a good day, and she longed for the peace of the wide pastures and thick woods of the Cross R Ranch.

The ride back proved much easier than she'd expected. Nimblefoot was calm and willing, suiting his pace to that of the other horses and not stumbling at all. Gypsy, perhaps a little tired from the long ride, was also quiet, trotting and loping at Nimblefoot's side like a sorrel shadow. Even so, Wendy felt better when the barn and house came into sight and the ride was completely over.

Uncle Art came out to greet them, his quick

questions about Nimblefoot making it clear that he had been worried through the long day. Wendy said as little as possible, taking her time with the unsaddling, then getting a brush and currycomb to groom both the gelding and Gypsy. Her aunt and uncle moved around, feeding the horses still in the barn and grooming the horse her aunt had ridden.

Uncle Art came over as she gave Nimblefoot's lead rope to Gypsy and said, "Take him to the corral, Gypsy."

"Gypsy is better than a dog," he said with a chuckle as the filly led the gelding to the gate. "By the time she's old enough to ride, she'll be ready to take over our training program." Then he sobered and said, "Laura mentioned Nimblefoot's trouble, Wendy."

"I think it's just that he's afraid," Wendy said, rubbing the gelding's shining hide before she turned him into the big corral. "He was fine coming home."

"Over easy ground."

"If his shoulder was stiff or hurt, wouldn't it show up in other ways?" Wendy asked. "He turns

78

and runs fine, and even the grass is rough in spots, too."

"I'm going to have Dr. James check him, just to be sure." He sighed. "It might be better if it turned out to be physical, Wendy. There could be exercises or something that would help. If it's in his mind, I don't know that anything will help."

"There has to be a way." Wendy spoke firmly, but she wasn't reassured when Uncle Art didn't argue. They fed the horses in silence.

Wendy had planned on riding Nimblefoot out into the north pasture the next day, but they had barely returned from church when someone began honking a car horn out in front. "They're early," Aunt Laura said, tossing her gloves, hat, and purse onto the kitchen table and hurrying back out the door to the garage. Wendy followed, curious.

The man and woman who stepped out of the car were smiling and friendly, but the boy in the backseat didn't even speak. Mrs. Webster drew Wendy and Aunt Laura away from the car and said, "I'm afraid Jimmy didn't want to come this year. He still hasn't gotten over that terrible fall."

Aunt Laura sighed. "We were hoping that he'd had a chance to ride in the city. Riding is the only cure, you know."

"You and the doctor!" Mrs. Webster sounded almost angry. "He just insisted that we come out here with Jimmy. I really don't see what difference it makes. I thought a beach vacation would be just as healthful."

"Now, Gloria," Mr. Webster said. "Jimmy, get out of the car and say hello to the Roushes and meet their niece, Wendy McLyon. We're going to be here for a month, so you'd better stop acting like a spoiled brat."

The boy got out slowly, his expression sulky. He was quite small and, Wendy thought, looked even younger than ten. "I'm not going to ride any dumb horses," he said.

"They aren't dumb," Wendy said. "I've got a filly that's smart enough to open gates and lead other horses around—and she's just a yearling."

Jimmy turned his back and stared into the car without another word. Wendy looked at her aunt but got only a slight shrug as an answer.

"Well, are you ready to move in?" Uncle Art asked, breaking the uncomfortable silence.

"Same cabin?" Mrs. Webster asked, red spots of embarrassment in her cheeks.

The flurry of moving them in and then preparing a proper Sunday dinner kept everyone busy. It wasn't till late afternoon that Wendy was alone with Aunt Laura and could ask, "What are we going to do with them for a whole month if Jimmy's going to be such a brat?"

"I've been thinking about that," Aunt Laura said, "and I'm not sure that it's exactly the way it looks."

"What do you mean?"

"Jimmy was hurt in that fall, and I think he honestly believes that it was Nimblefoot's fault—and it could have been, you know." She waved aside the hot protests that rose to Wendy's lips and went on without giving her a chance to speak. "Anyway, that doesn't matter—the fault, I mean. To Jimmy, Nimblefoot is a horse that tried to hurt him."

"Nimblefoot nearly died because of that fall," Wendy reminded her.

Her aunt nodded. "A less spoiled child would have thought of that, but Jimmy was whisked away without ever seeing Nimblefoot. Now he's just a child who fell off a horse and didn't have to get back on. He's had a whole year to remember the pain and the fear, and he has that excuse to keep him from wanting to ride again."

"Are you trying to tell me that he's really afraid to ride?" Wendy asked.

"I think if we can get him on a horse again, he'll forget his fear of them in a hurry."

"Good luck," Wendy said with a touch of sympathy. Though she couldn't really forgive Jimmy for his hard attitude toward horses, she did understand how his fear might have come about.

"I don't think either Art or I can do it," Aunt Laura said.

"Well, then how. . . ." Wendy's voice trailed off as she realized what her aunt was hinting at. "You think I can do it?"

"I think you're our best hope." Aunt Laura smiled. "Try anyway, okay? He's really not such a brat when you get to know him."

"I'll do what I can," Wendy said, though she

had grave doubts about her ability to help Jimmy. As far as she could see, she was going to have her hands full just trying to save Nimblefoot, without worrying about the boy who was at least partially responsible for what had happened to the troubled horse.

7 · *Thieves*

BY THE TIME Jimmy and the Websters left the living room and retired to their cabin that evening, Wendy had more doubts than ever. Jimmy had rejected every offer of friendship, refusing to watch the working of the yearlings, scarcely speaking to George and Cliff, who had returned in time for the Sunday night cold buffet, and generally ignoring any mention of horses or riding.

"We might as well turn the yearlings out tomorrow," Uncle Art said as Wendy helped with the feeding, "except for Gypsy, of course. The four older horses will be enough to work while we've got people in the cabins. Do you think you could herd them down to the lake pasture for me, Wendy?"

"Be glad to," Wendy said, thinking that it would give her a chance to ride Nimblefoot alone.

"See if you can talk Jimmy into going along, too," he added. "The sooner we get him on a horse, the better."

"I'll try," she said without enthusiasm. The last person she wanted along when she was testing Nimblefoot was Jimmy; she remembered all too well—and with distaste—what he'd said when he happened to glimpse Nimblefoot in the big corral.

"What are you keeping that killer horse for, Mr. Roush?" he'd asked. "I thought you were going to shoot him."

Her uncle's gentle words about the gelding's suffering and slow recovery from the fall had done nothing to soften Jimmy's attitude, and he'd gone to his cabin still muttering that Nimblefoot was dumb and mean and should be shot for what he'd done.

Still, a promise was a promise, so right after breakfast, Wendy took Jimmy aside and asked, "How would you like to help me drive the yearlings out to the south pasture, Jimmy?"

"No, thanks. I don't want to chase a bunch of

dumb horses." His words were sullen, but behind them Wendy sensed a bit of doubt and loneliness.

"Not even if we come home by way of a haunted canyon?" Wendy asked and was rewarded with a quick glow of interest.

"What haunted canyon?" Jimmy asked, following her as she headed for the corrals.

"Haven't you ever heard of Gulligan Gulch?" she asked, then spent the next few minutes telling him the same tale that Carol and Kirk had told her.

"Is it too far to walk?" Jimmy asked when she finished.

"Well, I don't know," Wendy hedged, "but we have to ride there today because of the yearlings. It's much too far by way of the lake pasture."

"Couldn't I meet you there?" he asked, looking hopeful.

"You have to ride, Jimmy. There's nothing to do on a ranch if you don't. Ladybug isn't mean; you know that. She wouldn't hurt you."

"I don't want to ride Ladybug," Jimmy said, turning away from the corral angrily. "I don't want to ride any horse, and I don't care if I never

86

see Gulligan Gulch." He went stomping off toward the cabin without looking back.

"No luck?" Uncle Art asked, stepping out of the shadowed doorway of the barn.

"Not a bit," Wendy said. "I even told him I'd take him to Gulligan Gulch if he'd ride with me, but. . . ."

"You what?" Her uncle's look was disapproving. "Why did you tell him that?"

"Well, I just— Well, Kirk and Carol took me there the day before the Saddle Club ride, and I thought it was interesting and would appeal to a boy Jimmy's age. He was interested, too, but not enough to ride there."

"That's not a place I want our guests going, Wendy," Uncle Art said.

"Why not?"

"It's dangerous. The old cabin should be torn down and—" He paused. "Did you take Nimblefoot into that gulch?"

"No. I told you he refused to go on the trail. We left all the horses up in the trees, but then Gypsy followed us down. . . ." Wendy hesitated, then said, "I'm sorry if you don't approve of my going there. I didn't know that when Carol and Kirk suggested that we explore the place."

"I'm sorry I growled," Uncle Art said. "I've no objection to your going there, as long as you're careful. It's Jimmy I was worried about. Boys his age have been known to get into trouble in places like the Gulch. That's why I rarely mention it to the guests that come here."

"Well, I didn't tell him it was within walking distance," Wendy said, "so I doubt that you'll have to worry about Jimmy exploring it."

Uncle Art's arm was warm on her shoulders as he said, "Let's just forget it. I should have warned you before, and anyway, no harm done. Want to give the yearlings one last workout before you and Gypsy turn them loose to play for the rest of the summer?"

Wendy spent the morning working the yearlings and playing with Gypsy, allowing the filly to lead each colt or filly to and from the corral, and rewarding her for her efforts with praise and petting. The only things that bothered her were Jimmy, sitting by himself on the front porch of the house watching, without a smile, and Nimblefoot's occasional whicker to tell her that he, too, would like to join in the fun.

"Do you realize it's almost lunchtime?" Uncle Art asked when Gypsy had led the last colt back to the corral.

"My stomach does," Wendy said with a chuckle. "I guess I'd better get inside and help Aunt Laura, now that we have guests to serve."

"You'll have to start changing before meals, too," Uncle Art said with a grin. "Most of our guests aren't too fond of the horsy smell, even though I keep telling Laura that it's authentic Western flavor."

"I'd better do that first then," Wendy said, sighing, for she knew she'd be riding out with the yearlings right after lunch. "I might ruin their appetites."

Before she reached her room, however, Aunt Laura came out of the kitchen and asked, "Wendy, have you been taking cans of peaches with you when you ride or hike?"

"What?" Wendy blinked at her for a moment, then shook her head. "Nothing but sandwiches— oh, and apples or carrots for Gypsy. Why?"

"Well, when I made my supply list Friday, I didn't put peaches on it because I thought I had four cans, but when I started to make my ginger-bread and peach dessert, there wasn't a single can on the garage shelves."

"Do you suppose Cliff and George could have taken them out to the bunkhouse or something?" Wendy suggested.

"Not without mentioning it. Besides, they were gone most of the weekend. Art says he didn't eat them while we were gone Saturday." She shook her head. "It's not that the peaches are particularly important; it's just that I've never had food disappear that way before. I could swear I'm short some other things, too."

"Like what?" Wendy asked, her washing and changing forgotten.

"I can't be sure, but I thought I had three loaves of bread left from the last batch I baked, and I found only two. The peanut butter is gone and . . . I don't know. Maybe I'm just getting old and forgetful."

"If you are, you're not alone," Uncle Art said, coming out in a clean shirt and pants, his hair plastered down damply. "I seem to have misplaced a couple of horse blankets."

"Do you think we have a thief?" Aunt Laura asked.

"I don't want to," Uncle Art answered, then added, "I don't know who it could be, anyway. There are no strangers in the area—not that I've seen."

"Well, there's no time to worry about it now," Aunt Laura said, turning back to the kitchen. "Hurry and change, Wendy. We're about ready to eat."

The thought of a thief in the area troubled Wendy all during lunch, though neither her aunt nor her uncle mentioned it again. She found herself studying Jimmy. Because she resented him and his attitude toward Nimblefoot, she could almost believe that he might be the one; yet she could see no reason for such actions.

After lunch she changed back into her riding clothes and walked down to the corral with Uncle Art and a rather reluctant Jimmy. "Sure you won't change your mind about going with me, Jimmy?" she asked. "It's a perfect day for a ride."

"Don't you want to see the rest of the new foals?" Uncle Art asked. "Wendy's going to be taking Dotted Doll and her little colt out, too, now that he's old enough to join the herd."

"I don't want to look at a bunch of dumb horses," Jimmy said. Then he looked up at Uncle Art. "I'd like to walk to Gulligan Gulch," he said. "Where is it, Mr. Roush?"

"It's out that way," Uncle Art said, waving a negligent hand in the direction of the north pasture, "but it's a long hike, and you probably couldn't find it, anyway."

"Somebody did," Jimmy said defiantly.

"What do you mean?" Uncle Art asked, stopping so suddenly that Wendy nearly bumped into him.

"I saw smoke out that way this morning."

"Are you sure?" Uncle Art asked, his eyes narrowing as he questioned the boy.

"It was out that way." Jimmy pointed. Wendy stared in that direction.

"I don't see anything now," Uncle Art said, but Wendy could tell that he was troubled. "Maybe it was just some dust or a cloud or something."

"It was someone hiding out in the gulch," Jimmy said, "like cattle rustlers or robbers, or maybe even the ghost of Gulligan, like Wendy says."

"That was just a story," Wendy assured him quickly, her eyes meeting her uncle's in apology. "I guess I'd better get going," she added, heading for the barn to get Nimblefoot's bridle.

Uncle Art talked to Jimmy for a moment more, then left the boy and came to help Wendy saddle the gelding. "Do you think you could come home by the gulch?" he asked in a low voice. "Just ride along the top and check for signs of smoke."

"Sure I will," Wendy answered, not mentioning the fact that she had planned that from the beginning. "Do you really think Jimmy saw something out there?"

He shrugged. "It's hard to tell with him, but I wouldn't want to take a chance. There's always the possibility that someone might be in the shack." He paused, then added, "That's another reason I don't want you down in the gulch alone. Just stay on the rim today, okay?"

"Surely you don't believe the cattle rustler

93

theory," Wendy teased as she opened the gate of the small corral and released Gypsy. Then she rode in to drive the yearlings out. Sad whinnies rose in a chorus as the three two-year-olds and the one three-year-old filly watched the younger horses trot away.

"Don't be too long," Uncle Art called after her as he released the Appaloosa mare Dotted Doll and her gangling colt. "I've asked Dr. James to stop by late this afternoon to check Nimblefoot's shoulder."

Wendy waved in answer, but her heart stopped at the words. Ever since Aunt Laura had mentioned the possibility that Nimblefoot's problems could be physical, she'd been dreading the moment when she'd have to find out for sure.

She tried not to think of it as she maneuvered her small herd of horses through the gate and into the lake pasture. Now she would take Nimblefoot back toward Gulligan Gulch and see how he behaved. Then perhaps she would know better what to say to the veterinarian.

It took only a short time to find the herd, and Wendy didn't waste much time watching the yearlings and Dotted Doll as they galloped across the meadow to join the other horses. She turned Nimblefoot away and whistled for Gypsy, calling the filly back from the herd. Her nerves were already taut as she headed for the gate to the north pasture, wondering what she would find there.

8 · *Letters From the Past*

WENDY HAD no trouble following the trail she'd ridden Friday with Kirk and Carol, but this time she paid little attention to anything but the horse. At first Nimblefoot was fine, acting no different than he had in the lake pasture. Then they reached the first rocky ground. Loose shale rattled under his hooves—and he stumbled.

"What is it, boy?" Wendy asked, reining in at once. Nimblefoot stood quietly, and after a few minutes, she started forward again, staying at a walk, her eyes on the ground. The turf was rough and uneven, but tough prairie grass covered it now, and Nimblefoot moved along without any difficulty.

As she rode through the trees, Wendy caught

sight of a deep cut and, after a moment's figuring, decided that it must be the end of Gulligan Gulch. Riding closer, she confirmed her conclusion by spotting the small stream that flowed out of the cut to join the main stream that meandered through most of the Cross R.

"I'd like to ride you in there," Wendy said to the horse. "Maybe if you went through the bottom of the gulch, you wouldn't be so afraid." However, her uncle's warning had been clear, and Wendy turned the gelding away from the cut, riding instead along the grassy flanks of the rising mountains.

Remembering Jimmy's story, she looked around for signs of fire damage, but there was nothing to be seen. The area was peaceful in the early afternoon sun, and Wendy found herself relaxing a little as the gelding and Gypsy plodded along. Then Nimblefoot stumbled again, his hooves rattling on some rock.

Wendy leaned forward, her eyes on the ground ahead. She guided him carefully, trying to go from one patch of grass to another, without crossing any of the bare spots where wind and snow had stripped the soil away and left the mountain's rocky ribs exposed. Nimblefoot moved less surely, but he seemed to stumble only when they were forced to cross a section of rock.

Her heart ached for the horse as she felt the sweat of fear rising on his shoulders, yet she knew she couldn't turn back. Finally, as they neared the crest of the ridge, where the trail to the gulch began, Nimblefoot's fear became too strong, and she could feel his shudders even through the saddle leather.

"Let's see if it helps if I get down, fella," she said, stopping the horse and dismounting, much to Gypsy's joy. The filly, who'd stayed close to Nimblefoot's side, now stepped out, grabbing the bridle reins and trotting ahead.

Wendy started to call out to her, then deliberately closed her mouth as she watched the two horses. Surprisingly enough, Nimblefoot wasn't fighting Gypsy's lead, even though she took him across a ridge of rock. He stumbled and bounced a bit oddly, but he didn't stop until they reached the trees and the first curve of the trail down into Gulligan Gulch. Wendy hurried after them.

Curious, Wendy examined the gelding's shoulder, then ran her hand down his leg, and finally picked up his hoof. Though he was still wet with nervousness, there was no sign that anything was wrong . . . no swelling, no wincing away from her fingers.

"You need shoes, Nimblefoot," Wendy said, after examining his hooves. "If I'm going to be riding you regularly, we don't want to take a chance on having your hooves crack and split."

Nimblefoot nuzzled her arm, then followed her for a few steps as she walked toward the gulch trail, stopping only when she reached the first rocky ledge. Wendy kept him there for a few minutes, then led him back to where the grass was thick before she mounted and turned him toward home.

She felt a little better at what she'd discovered, for she was almost sure now that it was rock that made Nimblefoot stumble—not because it was uneven or because he had some hidden weakness, but simply because he was afraid of stepping on rock.

She was nearly through the north pasture when

100

a small figure came out of the trees. Wendy reined in sharply. "Jimmy," she gasped, recognizing the boy, "what are you doing out here?"

"Looking for the robbers," he said, moving back from Nimblefoot as the horse extended his nose toward him.

"What robbers? There's no one out here." Wendy spoke firmly. "What are you talking about?"

"Someone stole my jacket."

"What? When did that happen?"

"Last night or yesterday, after we got here. It was in the car when we came, and now it's gone." He glared at her, his jaw set. "Don't tell me there aren't any robbers, either. I heard your uncle talking about some missing horse blankets, too."

"Don't be silly," Wendy said. "Your mother or dad probably took the jacket out of the car for you, that's all."

Jimmy shook his head, looking stubborn. "It was stolen, and the robbers are hiding in the gulch."

"Then you'd just better stay away from there, don't you think?" Wendy asked. "They're liable

101

to get you." She started to touch the gelding with her heels, then stopped to ask, "Want to ride double with me?"

"I wouldn't ride that horse if I had to walk a million miles," Jimmy said.

"Just don't go out into the north pasture alone," Wendy said over her shoulder. She hurried Nimblefoot into a lope; she had spotted a car parked by the barn and was pretty sure that it belonged to Dr. James.

"Well, well," Dr. James said as she stopped Nimblefoot in front of him. "He certainly looks sound."

"I'm sure he is," Wendy said, starting to get down.

"No, no, stay on him for a minute," Dr. James said. "I'd like to see you work him a little. Lope him in some figure eights, will you? And make them smaller each time."

"Let me catch Gypsy and hold her," Uncle Art said, hurrying forward to catch the filly's halter. "No use trying to watch eight legs instead of four." He led Gypsy aside.

For the next fifteen minutes, Wendy gave Nimblefoot a thorough workout before the two watching men. The gelding moved as easily and sure-footedly as any horse she'd ever ridden, and later, when the vet ran his experienced hands over the scarred shoulder, Nimblefoot didn't shy away at all.

"What do you think?" Uncle Art asked when Dr. James straightened up.

"I wish all my patients healed as well."

Wendy grinned, but her happiness faded as her uncle asked, "Then why does he stumble on rocky ground, Doc?"

The vet shrugged, his eyes on Wendy. "What do you think?" he asked. "You've been riding him, haven't you?"

Wendy nodded. "I don't know exactly, except that it's not uneven or rough ground that makes him stumble; it's just bare rock. He walks funny on it and tries to go around it if he can. Today I rode him near Gulligan Gulch, and I watched. If I kept him on the turf, he didn't stumble, but the minute his hooves touched the rocky places. . . ." She shrugged. "Why would that be, Dr. James?"

The vet pondered for a moment, then shook his head. "He fell on a rock trail, didn't he?"

Uncle Art nodded.

"Then there must be a connection in his mind. He was badly hurt on rock. Every time he crosses rock now, he feels insecure, I suppose."

"But what can I do about it?" Wendy asked, quite sure that the veterinarian was right in his diagnosis.

Now Dr. James shrugged. "That's not easy to say, Wendy. I can treat most physical problems a horse or any other animal has, but the ones in their minds are something else. I think he just needs to regain his confidence in his own sure-footedness, but I have no idea how it can be done— or even if it can." His kind face was shadowed as he added, "You know, too, that he'll be a constant danger to his rider till he does get better."

Wendy nodded. "I won't let anyone else ride him," she said firmly, "and I'll be careful."

"You haven't any suggestions?" Uncle Art asked. "Isn't there something that might help?"

"Well, you might try turning him into a gymkhana horse," Dr. James said. "If he does well in

104

that kind of maneuvering, it ought to build his confidence."

"Wouldn't that be dangerous, too?" Uncle Art asked. "If he stumbles and falls in the arena—"

"Unless you've got a rock arena, I don't think you need to worry," Wendy said.

"Why don't you see how he acts at the practice?" Dr. James asked. "If he doesn't work out, that's time enough to think about destroying him." He reached out to pet Nimblefoot's neck. "He's such a good little horse, it would be a shame to give up without trying everything possible to cure him."

Wendy swallowed hard and said, "If you don't think I can handle him, Uncle Art, I'm sure that Carol or Kirk would be willing to try working with him. Maybe a more experienced rider. . . ."

Her uncle's expression softened. "He means that much to you, Wendy?" he asked.

She nodded, unable to speak around the lump in her throat. Nimblefoot nuzzled her arm as if he understood, and she had to blink back her tears.

"When is the first practice?" her uncle asked

105

with a sigh that revealed his worry.

"Tomorrow afternoon, I think," Dr. James said. "Kirk was talking about it this morning while he helped me with Pete Foster's milk cow. She got herself into some wire, and we had a devil of a time getting her loose in one piece." The vet grinned. "Guess I'm getting too old to handle them."

"You'll be handling animals when I'm too old to get on a horse," Uncle Art said with a chuckle. "Right now, come on up to the house and help me reduce Laura's cookie supply." He started toward the house, then turned back for a moment to ask, "Did you find anything up near the gulch, Wendy?"

Wendy shook her head, then added, "Nothing except Jimmy. He was about halfway there. Said his jacket was missing, and he thought the robbers in the gulch had stolen it."

Her uncle sighed and headed for the house, calling, "Come up when you get the horse put away. Laura's been baking cookies all afternoon, and they smell delicious."

Wendy nodded but took her time grooming and

106

talking to Gypsy and Nimblefoot. Though she was relieved by the veterinarian's verdict, she also realized that he was leaving it solely up to her to solve Nimblefoot's problem.

"Take him to the corral, Gypsy," Wendy said, handing the filly Nimblefoot's lead rope. She laughed aloud at the serious, businesslike way the filly trotted out with the gelding in tow. If only Nimblefoot had Gypsy's confidence, she thought sadly. Then she brightened slightly as she remembered that, just a few months ago, Gypsy had been shy and half-wild.

Could she do it again? she asked herself, turning the two horses into the corral. She headed for the house, her stomach rumbling eagerly for the promised cookies. Having Gypsy for her own had been almost a miracle. Could she really expect another one for Nimblefoot? She opened the kitchen door.

"Hey, you got a couple of letters today," Aunt Laura called as she pulled a cookie sheet out of the oven. "I put them on your study table."

"Save me some cookies," Wendy said. "I'll go wash the horses off my hands." She hurried through the dining room and into the hall to her own room, sure that the letters would be from her father and anxious to know what he had to say about her getting Gypsy for her own.

She smiled ruefully as she reached for the letters, wondering what he would think when the slow mails brought him her last letter, the one about Nimblefoot. Then she forgot everything as she recognized the handwriting on the top letter. It was from Gretchen Simpson!

A mixture of feelings rushed over her, and she had to sit down on the white chair before she could even pick up the envelope. Gretchen had been her best friend when she lived in Phoenix. They had shared riding lessons and a deep love of the horses that Gretchen's father kept in his riding stable.

For a moment Wendy felt the warmth of those memories, but then her anger flared as she remembered Gretchen's betrayal. After the accident, after Buck had been killed by her carelessness, Gretchen had turned away, had never even spoken to her again. Gretchen had blamed her for killing Buck, and their friendship had ended.

All the old hurt and anger came back. Wendy put the unopened envelope down and picked up the letter from her father instead. She took her time reading it, but all the while, a part of her mind was still on the other letter, curious to know what Gretchen had to say now. Finally, unable to stand it, she opened the letter, spread out the single sheet of paper, and began to read.

Dear Wendy:

I know you probably want to tear this up without reading it, and I don't blame you. Right after your accident happened, I thought it was all your fault, that you'd killed Buck because you wouldn't listen to the stablemen. I never wanted to speak to you again, but that was a long time ago, and now I feel different.

The day you came to school, I was ashamed of myself. I wanted to say I was sorry for not coming to the hospital to see you, but you left before I could.

Well, anyway, I called your apartment a dozen times, but there was never any answer. Then finally your father told me that you were gone.

Wendy leaned back and closed her eyes for a moment, remembering the long days in the apartment . . . days when she hadn't answered the telephone or the doorbell . . . days when she had wanted to die for what she had done to Buck. It was a while before she opened her eyes and read the last paragraph.

> Anyway, I guess what I'm trying to say is that I'm sorry and I miss you, and I'd like it very much if you'd write and tell me what it's like living there. Please.
>
> Love,
Gretchen

Wendy refolded the letter and put it back in the envelope, but she didn't get up. Instead she turned and stared out of her window at the trees that separated the ranch house from the highway. She thought about Gretchen and all that had happened in the months since the accident, and her anger and hurt began to fade.

Tonight, she thought as she got up and went to wash and change her clothes. Tonight she would write and tell Gretchen all about Gypsy and Nimblefoot and the Saddle Club and the new friends she was making here. *And*, she added to herself, *I'll ask Gretchen all about what's going on in Phoenix.* She went out to the kitchen feeling much better.

110

9 · *Getting in Practice*

THE EVENING passed quietly enough as she wrote letters, first to Gretchen, then to her father. It helped a little to write about Nimblefoot, putting his problems into perspective and thinking about them logically instead of wanting to cry every time she thought of failure.

By the time she went to bed, she was more determined than ever. Though she'd never seen a gymkhana, she was going to make Nimblefoot the best gymkhana horse anyone had ever known!

At breakfast the next morning, George said, "Want to help me put shoes on that gelding, Wendy?"

"Are you a blacksmith, too?" Wendy asked, impressed.

"Working on a ranch all my life, I've learned to do a little of everything," George said with a grin. "Besides, we've got too many horses on this ranch to have a blacksmith out to do the work." Then he sobered. "Nimblefoot may need a friendly hand, though."

"He's not hard to shoe, is he?" Uncle Art asked.

"Wasn't before," George said, "but he was hurting bad when I pulled his shoes for Dr. James, and horses remember things like that. I'll take my time, though, and see if we can get through it without a battle."

"Why did you have to pull his shoes after the fall?" Wendy asked, her thoughts fastening on this new fact.

"They were torn loose, and one of his hooves was cut up inside from the fall." George shook his head. "He was a pitiful sight, Wendy. None of us thought he'd make it."

"He should have been shot," Jimmy said from the doorway. "He wanted to hurt me, and he'll hurt you, too, Wendy. He's mean."

"That's not so, Jimmy," Wendy said after an anxious glance at her uncle.

112

"Are your folks up yet, Jimmy?" Aunt Laura asked, getting up from the table.

"They're still asleep." As he spoke, Jimmy sniffed the air like a hungry dog.

"Well, then, why don't you eat with us?" Aunt Laura suggested. "Let me fix you a plate."

Though Wendy could have done without him, Jimmy stayed with her through the morning, even standing around watching while George and Uncle Art put new shoes on Nimblefoot. He actually seemed disappointed when the gelding remained calm through the shoeing. When it was finished, he asked, "Why did you put shoes on him, Mr. Roush? I thought he was just going to run around here."

"Wendy's going to be riding him in the gymkhanas, we hope, so he'll need shoes. All our riding horses have to be shod. You remember that from last year, don't you?"

"He'll buck you off," Jimmy said, ignoring Uncle Art's words as he turned to Wendy. "You just wait."

"Why don't you come out to the practice with us?" Uncle Art suggested. "See for yourself how

Nimblefoot behaves when he's ridden."

For a moment Wendy hoped that the boy would refuse, but Jimmy's eyes brightened at the suggestion. "Could I really?" he asked.

"Ask your folks," Uncle Art said. He turned to Wendy as Jimmy ran off toward the cabin. "I know he rubs you the wrong way, honey," he said, "but he is a guest, and we've got to do our best to change his mind about horses."

"I don't think he'll ever change his mind about Nimblefoot," Wendy said bitterly.

Her uncle frowned. "I don't know. I don't think he'd hate him so much if he hadn't really loved him first. It's sort of like what you told us about your friend Gretchen last night; neither of you would have been so hurt or angry if you hadn't been so close before the accident, would you?"

"But he actually wants Nimblefoot to fail," Wendy protested.

"Not as much as you want him to succeed," her uncle said with a grin, "and I'm betting on you."

Wendy relaxed a little. "How do we get to the gymkhana practice?" she asked. "Is it too far to ride there?"

114

Uncle Art nodded. "We'll take the pickup and horse trailer. The Saddle Club grounds are just this side of Littleville. You remember where we went to the Saddle Club meeting?"

Wendy whistled for Gypsy, who had been bouncing around as an audience to the horseshoeing. "Are you going to take another horse with us?" she asked, hoping her question sounded casual.

"I hadn't planned on it. Why?" Uncle Art looked puzzled. Then suddenly he smiled. "Gypsy?" he asked.

"Well, she does seem to have a good effect on Nimblefoot," Wendy answered quickly, returning his smile.

He laughed. "Besides, she is the official mascot of the Junior Saddle Club," he added for her. "All right, she can come, too. We'll teach her not to be afraid to ride in a horse trailer."

The rest of the morning passed quickly, and Wendy changed into clean riding clothes before lunch, knowing that they'd be leaving as soon as she had helped Aunt Laura with the dishes. "Are you going with us?" she asked her aunt as they carried the food into the dining room, where they were all eating.

"I'd love to," she said, "but the Websters thought that, as long as Jimmy was going with you, they'd like to ride down to the lake for a while. You know, they haven't been able to do any riding because Jimmy won't get on a horse."

"Maybe if they'd leave him, he'd be more willing to try," Wendy suggested, her dislike of the boy plain in her tone.

Aunt Laura laughed. "If they'd been more willing to let him alone, he wouldn't be so spoiled now. How are you doing with him?"

Wendy giggled. "Don't ask," she said with an exaggerated sigh.

"Well, they've only been here a few days," Aunt Laura said. "Maybe things will get better."

"Don't count on it," Wendy said without much enthusiasm.

The afternoon began poorly when Wendy tried to lead Nimblefoot into the trailer. He followed willingly enough till his hooves touched the ramp. Then he leaped back, dragging her with him. Wendy held the rope and tried talking to the

116

gelding, soothing him, before leading him forward again. He repeated his performance the moment his hooves touched the ramp.

"What's the matter with him, Uncle Art?" Wendy asked.

Her uncle shrugged. "He used to load without even being led," he said.

"What'll we do?"

"Try putting Gypsy in first," he suggested.

Wendy reached for Gypsy's lead, but the filly was ahead of her. Very sedately, she caught Nimblefoot's lead rope in her teeth and trotted toward the ramp. Wendy started forward, then stopped as Uncle Art moved ahead of her. Gypsy walked up the ramp and into one stall of the trailer, stopping only when Nimblefoot's rope tightened.

"Get in there," Uncle Art said, slapping Nimblefoot's black and white haunches. The gelding jumped, rocking the trailer a bit but somehow scrambling into the other stall. Uncle Art lifted the ramp quickly, to keep either horse from backing out. He grinned at Wendy. "Maybe a *horse* horse trainer isn't such a bad idea," he said.

117

Though Wendy had worried about it, Nimblefoot offered no problem when he was unloaded
at the Saddle Club arena, and she found Jimmy's
remarks about the dangers of riding him easy to
ignore. Once Gypsy was tied to the arena fence,
Wendy mounted Nimblefoot and rode over to
join Kirk and Carol.

It was fun sitting on the horses, listening to
everyone's gymkhana stories, discussing the practice, and telling her friends about the last few
days. All too soon, however, one of the women
from the Saddle Club was calling them into the
arena and explaining that each rider would be
given a chance to try the pole-bending and that
they should divide into groups of four, since there
were four lines of poles.

Carol, Kirk, Wendy, and a slender blond girl
named Betty were in the second group, and
Wendy could feel her nervousness rising as she
turned Nimblefoot to face the line of six evenly
spaced poles. "Just go slow the first time through,"
Carol counseled. "Quito and I will be in the next
line, and this is his first time, too, so we don't want
to knock any poles down. Don't start racing

118

your horse until you're certain he knows what he's doing."

Wendy nodded, her eyes on the first group as they wove down the line of poles the first time, turned a tight curve at the far end of the arena, wove back, made another tight turn for a third trip through the poles, then ended with a grand dash back to the finish line. It looked simple enough, if only Nimblefoot wouldn't stumble or get nervous. She held her breath as her group lined up for their turn.

Nimblefoot leaped forward at the starting gun and was into the poles before Wendy was ready, but she managed to stay aboard as he twisted between the broomsticks set in buckets of sand. She had little to do except to guide him into the turn for the second run through, and again for the third time.

It wasn't till she had made the final spin and started the race for the finish that she realized she and Nimblefoot were clearly ahead of the other horses, even Kirk's experienced Apache. They crossed the chalk finish line in fine shape.

"I thought this was your first gymkhana practice," Kirk said as he and Apache galloped up.

"It is," Wendy said, "but Nimblefoot seems to know what he's doing."

"If he's got something wrong with his shoulder, I wish Quito would catch it," Carol teased as she joined them. "I think we've got some real competition this year, Kirk."

"If he does other things as well as he does the poles, I may have to find another hobby," Kirk said, pretending to brood unhappily.

"It's beginner's luck," Wendy said as they rode over to take their places at the end of the line of riders, first pausing at the arena fence to pat Gypsy.

"Looks like you've got a gymkhana horse," Uncle Art said, seeming very pleased.

"He acts as if he knows what he's doing," Wendy said. "Did you ever use him in a gymkhana? You must have."

He started to shake his head, then snapped his fingers. "The first year I had him, one of the girls who worked for us rode him, and I think she did bring him to a few practice sessions. Then she got a horse of her own, and Nimblefoot didn't get any more workouts that summer."

"Well, he sure has a good memory," Wendy said, turning him into line.

"Have you heard about the robberies?" Kirk asked.

"What robberies?" Wendy asked, her thoughts turning at once to the trouble they'd had at the Cross R.

"The last few days, people all around our area have been reporting stuff missing," Carol said. "We've had blankets stolen and some food. The people across the road from you lost a ham, and Johnsons, on the other side, lost a number of small things, too."

"Have you missed anything on your place?" Kirk asked.

Wendy nodded, suddenly conscious of Jimmy standing nearby, just on the other side of the fence. "A couple of horse blankets and some food," she admitted.

"And my jacket," Jimmy added firmly. "It's the robbers hiding out in Gulligan Gulch. They're going to rob the bank in town, but they're stealing things now, while they wait for the right time."

122

"More than likely, it's someone passing through the country without any money," Kirk said. "Someone hungry and needing clothes or blankets to keep warm."

Wendy nodded her agreement, but Jimmy didn't seem to be listening. She was glad when they moved toward the head of the line again. The excitement of guiding Nimblefoot through the poles could again claim her whole attention.

The afternoon passed rapidly as she rode Nimblefoot through the cloverleaf barrel racing maneuvers, then mastered the art of grabbing a stake out of one barrel and depositing it in another barrel while Nimblefoot was running at a full gallop. The barrel and stake race, as it was called, proved to be the most difficult, but she survived it with only one splinter from the wooden stakes.

"This is great," she said as she rode out of the arena with the others. "When is the next practice? Soon, I hope."

"Thursday," Kirk said. "We have to have it right away so everybody gets a chance to try all the events that we'll have in our first gymkhana. Next time, we'll practice three events—the keyhole,

123

the hurdles, and the ribbon race."

"What in the world . . ." Wendy began, but before she could ask for more details, Uncle Art came hurrying up.

"Come on, honey," he said. "Let's get loaded up and on our way. I've got some chores to do, and it's getting kind of late."

"When are you coming over?" Wendy asked, turning away reluctantly.

"Maybe tomorrow afternoon?" Carol said, looking questioningly at Kirk.

He nodded. "See you then," he said.

"Sorry to rush you," Uncle Art said as he turned Gypsy loose to follow Nimblefoot toward the trailer, "but with Laura on a trail ride, she's going to be needing help in the kitchen, too."

"Gosh, you should have just left me," Wendy said, sliding down and unsaddling the gelding. "I didn't mean for you to wait around here all afternoon."

"I wanted to see how he'd do," Uncle Art said.

"What do you think?" Wendy said as she shooed the filly into the trailer and turned to Nimblefoot.

124

"He looks like a natural, so far." Her uncle moved to help her, but Nimblefoot was ahead of them, dancing for a moment at the foot of the ramp, then leaping in once again.

Uncle Art sighed. "Well, he does get in, anyway," he said. "I just hope he never misses."

Wendy smiled, but her pleasure was slightly tarnished by Jimmy's pouting expression.

"He's a crazy horse," the boy said. "Just you wait. You'll see I'm right . . . right about a lot of things."

"Like what, Jimmy?" Uncle Art asked.

"You'll see when it happens," Jimmy said mysteriously. "I've warned everybody, but nobody listens."

"You mean about Nimblefoot and what happened to you?" Wendy asked, half-angry, half-curious.

Jimmy shook his head. "You'll all see when they . . . when it happens."

Wendy got into the pickup with a sigh of relief, realizing that the boy was talking about the mysterious robberies, not her horse. She thought of telling Uncle Art about Jimmy's theory, then

125

decided against it, sure that such a discussion would only make the boy more curious about Gulligan Gulch. Still, as they rode home through the late afternoon, she couldn't quite forget her own feelings when she had been down in the gulch and had seen that pile of strangely new gunnysacks and the dustless table.

10 · Secret of the Gulch

THOUGH SHE MANAGED to put thoughts of the spooky gulch out of her mind while she was doing her kitchen chores and helping to serve the evening meal, the idea of someone's hiding there bothered her again when the work slackened. Much as she had doubted Jimmy's tale of bank robbers or cattle rustlers, she could see that there might be a germ of truth in what he said. Someone could be using the old cabin for shelter.

The idea hadn't disappeared by morning, so as soon as the chores were done, Wendy got Nimblefoot and Gypsy out of the corral and led them into the barn where her uncle was fixing a stall gate. "Mind if I take a little ride?" she asked.

"Going far?" he asked.

Wendy shook her head. "I just thought I'd take Nimblefoot on some more rock and see if the gymkhana practice helped him any."

"Well, you be careful. Being good at one kind of work doesn't mean he'll be good at another."

"I won't be gone long," Wendy promised. "I'll help you with the two-year-olds when I get back."

"Why don't you ride over to the Carters?" her uncle suggested. "There's some rough territory in that direction, too."

"Carol and Kirk are coming over here this afternoon, if that's okay with you."

"Fine. Maybe you can scout out a trail for a picnic Saturday afternoon. The Boyds will be arriving Thursday, so we'll have to start planning more activities for guests." He sighed. "I was just hoping that we'd have Jimmy's problem solved before then."

"I'll invite him to come with us this afternoon," Wendy said reluctantly. "Maybe having Kirk along will help."

"Maybe." He didn't sound too encouraging.

Wendy rode out quickly, wanting to get away from the house and barn area before Jimmy came

128

out of his family's cabin and tried to follow her. This time she was taking the shortest route to the gulch. As she rode by Happy Warrior's paddock, the big black and white Appaloosa stallion whinnied at Gypsy and Nimblefoot. Wendy called a greeting that was lost in the answering whinnies.

The gate was just a few hundred yards north of the paddock, but once through it, it was easy to disappear into the trees. Wendy rode quickly, not looking back. Her concentration was on picking an easy route for Nimblefoot and speculating about what she might find when she reached the gulch. She was just beginning to have doubts about riding this way, when she reached the barren ridge where the trail into the gulch began.

Nimblefoot stopped dead, and Wendy could feel the shivering fear that went through him, telling her that nothing had changed. She slid down reluctantly, then led him forward slowly till they reached the beginning of the trail. There he stopped, refusing to move another step. Talking and petting stopped his shivering but didn't move him forward. Finally she simply left him, reins

129

trailing, and started down the rocky trail, with Gypsy behind her.

The silence was unbelievable. Gypsy's dainty hooves rattled loudly on the loose pebbles, and the echoes seemed to bounce off the walls. Wendy gritted her teeth, realizing that if there was someone down there, they might very well hear her approach and hide. It seemed to take forever to reach the last turn of the trail, where she could see the bottom of the gulch.

Just as they reached the point where she could see the heavy growth, a small, very dirty white dog came racing out, barking wildly. Gypsy skidded to a halt, as did Wendy, but before the dog reached them, a whistle cut through the stillness, calling the dog back. It turned and disappeared into the brush without another sound.

Wendy hesitated, shivers touching her spine. Someone was down here; that was certain. But who? And why? She had a feeling that she should turn around and go home immediately, but somehow she couldn't quite bring herself to leave without knowing. She picked her way down the last few feet of the trail, then headed at once into the

130

thick brush where the dog had disappeared.

Gypsy followed her, a bit more noisily, but there was nothing she could do about that. When she finally reached a hedge of wild roses, she sank to her knees and began carefully parting the lower branches so that she could see beyond them to the cabin. She had just cleared a narrow opening, when Gypsy crowded up behind her.

"See, Moppa, it's a wild horse," a boy's voice said. "Now, don't bark and scare it away."

For a moment, Wendy froze in fear as the young boy seemed to be looking in her direction. Then she realized that he must be staring at Gypsy, who was, of course, peering over the rose-bushes. The boy was kneeling beside the stream, several tin plates beside him on the ground, as though he had stopped in the midst of washing them.

Gypsy, excited by the sight of the boy and dog, pushed against Wendy's back as she tried to get closer, and Wendy felt herself falling forward. Rose thorns ripped at her as she tumbled through the hedge and into the open, across the stream from the boy.

For just a moment, their eyes met. Then he was on his feet, running toward the cabin. By the time she had pulled herself up, he had completely disappeared, as had the little dog.

Wendy stared toward the cabin, wondering what to do. Should she follow the boy and find out why he was down here? she asked herself. She was curious, but the spooky old cabin really hadn't been that attractive, even when she'd been with Carol and Kirk, and now. . . . She took her time bathing her scratches and gouges in the icy stream water.

The tin plates were still there, and after a few minutes, she picked them up and headed reluctantly toward the cabin. Before she reached the door, however, it opened, and an older boy stepped out.

"Where do you think you're going?" he asked angrily.

"Who are you?" Wendy asked, looking at him coldly in an effort to hide her nervousness, "and what are you doing down here?"

"We're living here." His words were icy.

"In that old cabin?" She couldn't hide her

shock, remembering the cabin's interior.

"It's a roof, at least." The brown eyes turned her way were hostile.

"But it's not safe. You can't stay here," Wendy protested, remembering what her uncle had said.

"Who are you?" the boy asked. "What business is it of yours whether we stay here or not?"

"I'm Wendy McLyon, and this is my uncle's ranch." Wendy felt better as Gypsy came trotting up to stand behind her.

"Are you going to tell him about us?" the boy asked warily.

"Who are you, and what are you doing here?" Wendy asked for the second time, her fear fading as she realized that the boy couldn't be much older than she was.

"I'm Joel Anders," the boy said. "Fred is my brother—the boy you saw by the stream. We're just camping here, that's all."

"Where are your folks?" Wendy sensed that something was wrong with his bold words. "Did they let you come here, on private property?"

"Sure they did," Joel said. "We didn't think anyone would mind. We haven't seen anyone

134

around this gulch till today."

Wendy considered the words for a moment, then shook her head. "I don't believe you," she said quietly. "You're not old enough to be camping down here alone."

"I'm fourteen."

"I think you'd better come back to the ranch with me and call your folks," Wendy went on. "I know my uncle won't want you staying down here. He says the cabin isn't safe, and—"

"No!" The shout came from the door of the cabin where the younger boy, Fred, stood holding the dog. "You can't make us go back. They'll kill Moppa."

"Shut up, Fred," Joel said. Wendy could see the worry in his face, too.

"Who's Moppa?" Wendy asked. Then she remembered what Fred had said by the stream. "You mean somebody wants to kill your dog?"

Fred gave his brother a sorrowful glance, then nodded. "They say there's no place to keep him, so he'll have to be. . . ."

Joel sighed. "You might as well come on inside," he said to Wendy none too graciously.

135

"Why can't you keep him?" Wendy asked when she was seated at the table, with Moppa sniffing happily around her ankles. "He's a darling little dog."

Joel and Fred exchanged glances, and Joel sighed again. "If you must know, we ran away from home two weeks ago. It took us almost a week to get here from Missoula. Then we found this place Thursday night, and we thought—"

"You're the ones who took the food and blankets, aren't you?" Wendy broke in, her eyes spotting the empty food cans and the pile of blankets in the corner.

Joel nodded. "We spent most of Friday out looking for supplies. We tried not to take too much from any one place."

"It gets so cold," Fred murmured. "Our money ran out, and we were afraid to look for any odd jobs for fear they'd send us back."

"Back to what?" Wendy asked. "Are your folks the ones who want to get rid of Moppa?"

Joel shook his head. "Heck, no. Dad bought him for us before he lost his job."

"Then why. . . ."

"Dad lost his job, and then he went to California to see if he couldn't find something," Fred said. "He said he'd send for us as soon as he had a steady job and could find us a house and everything. Meantime, Mom had her job in Missoula, and everything was okay." He stopped, and Wendy could hear the catch in his voice that hinted at tears.

"Mom was in a car wreck," Joel went on. "She's going to be in the hospital for a couple of months. We were doing okay, but the people from the court wouldn't let us stay there alone. They couldn't find Dad, so they were going to send me to Dad's cousin in Wyoming, and Aunt Biddy in Seattle was going to take Fred. Only nobody wanted Moppa and. . . ." His voice trailed off. Then he added, "That's why we split."

Wendy didn't say anything as she tried to absorb the facts he'd laid out for her. It was a sad mess, she thought bitterly, especially the part about getting rid of Moppa. She remembered all too well the pain she had felt when they had moved a few years before and she'd had to give away her kitten and puppy—and she had even known that they were getting good homes.

"You mean you were planning to hide here all summer?" she asked at last.

Joel nodded. "What else can we do?" he asked. "We figured to go back in a couple of months, about the time Mom will be getting out of the hospital. Then everything will be okay again."

"What about your mother?" Wendy asked. "She must be frantic with worry."

Joel shook his head. "We pretended to take the buses to Aunt Biddy and Cousin Jesse, so she thinks we're there. We wouldn't worry her while she's in the hospital."

Wendy looked worriedly around the single room. "You can't go on stealing supplies," she said. "Everybody is talking about it already, and someone is sure to catch you sooner or later."

Fred sighed. "Then we'll have to move on," he said, his tone quietly defiant. "I'm not going to let them take Moppa."

Wendy bent down to pet the rough-furred head, and the long pink tongue came out to caress her fingers. She didn't know what to say. Letting the boys hide here was wrong, she knew, and

138

Uncle Art would be furious if he found out; but sending them back wasn't right, either. The silence grew heavy.

"Are you going to tell on us?" Fred asked at last, his dark eyes pleading.

"I don't want to," Wendy admitted, "but you can't go on living this way."

"What else can we do?" Joel asked. "I don't want to steal, Wendy, but we have to eat and keep warm."

Wendy thought for a moment. Then a plan drifted into her thoughts. "Maybe we could help you," she said slowly.

"We?" Joel looked at her warily. "Who's 'we'?"

"My friends Carol Carter and Kirk Donahue. They live on ranches around here, and we ride together a lot."

His face didn't change. "What do you mean, 'help'?"

"Well, we're always going on picnics, so we could probably bring you food. That way you wouldn't have to steal, and then maybe nobody would find you."

"Would you do that?" Fred asked, looking

even younger as hope filled his thin, dark face.

"You mean you won't turn us over to the police?" Joel asked, more wary than his little brother.

"I'll have to ask Carol and Kirk, but if they agree and we can take care of you. . . ." Wendy watched anxiously as he thought about her idea. "It's better than getting caught stealing, isn't it?" she asked after a few minutes of silence.

The two boys exchanged glances, then finally nodded. "When will you talk to them?" Joel asked.

"This afternoon," Wendy said. "We're going riding together."

"Will you come by and tell us?" Fred asked. "I mean, if they won't do it, we'll have to leave befor they tell anybody."

"We'll all ride this way and talk to you," Wendy promised. Then, thinking more practically, she asked, "Do you have enough food for today and tonight?"

Joel nodded. "We've still got ham and bread and a little bit of peanut butter."

Wendy got up. "I'll see you later, then," she said, "and I really hope we can help."

"So do I," Joel said, smiling for the first time.

140

"And thanks, Wendy," he added.

Wendy waved, then hurried back to where Gypsy was happily grazing by the stream. As she started back up the steep trail to the top of the gulch, she was already planning ways to get food for the boys.

11 · Plotters

THOUGH THE SECRET bothered her when she faced her uncle and the others, Wendy held her tongue. She concentrated on working with Nimblefoot, then helped her Uncle Art with the training of the two-year-olds. She was glad when afternoon came and she could talk to Carol and Kirk about it.

"Those poor kids," Kirk said when she had finished. "What can we do to help them?"

Wendy outlined her picnic plan quickly, her heart warming at their immediate response to her feelings. It was like being back with Gretchen, in the good days before the accident.

"Is Joel bigger than I am?" Kirk asked.

Wendy studied him, then nodded. "Heavier and taller. He's fourteen and looks a little older."

"I think there's an old coat in the barn that might fit him," Carol said. "Let's ride over there and get it—and some food."

"What'll we tell your mother?" Wendy asked. "About the food, I mean."

"Nothing," Carol said. "She's in town at some church guild meeting. If she misses the food, she'll just figure we made a snack." She grinned. "Mom's not careful like your aunt. I mean, she just cooks for the three of us—and Ben Fisher, when he's helping Dad with the work—so she doesn't have to keep track of her supplies the way you folks do."

"I'm supposed to be finding a trail for a picnic ride Saturday," Wendy said. "Do you know what would be a good, easy route for Nimblefoot?"

"How about a cookout on the lakeshore?" Carol suggested. "We did that pretty often while I helped out last year. You go through the north pasture, but stay away from the real rocky area near the gulch." She looked at Kirk. "Know the way I mean?"

He nodded. "We can detour that way from Carol's place if we ride fast," he said to Wendy.

"Then you'll be able to describe it to your uncle."

Wendy nodded. "I really hate not telling him about Joel and Fred," she said, "but I can't help it. If I tell Uncle Art and Aunt Laura, I know they'll feel they have to tell the authorities, and then the boys will be sent away, and poor Moppa. . . ."

"We'll just have to take care of them," Carol said, urging Quito into a canter as they headed back toward the Carter ranch. "They should be safe from discovery as long as they stay in the gulch."

Though Wendy had her doubts, the next few days seemed to prove Carol's opinion to be correct. It took some tricky maneuvering and a few evasive answers to Uncle Art and Aunt Laura, but Wendy managed to make at least one trip a day to the gulch, always carrying food—a few apples, a bag of cookies, a couple of sandwiches, two or three eggs left hidden when she collected the rest from the chicken house, a loaf of bread, potatoes to bake—not to mention candles, matches, and an old sweater of Uncle Art's.

Kirk and Carol, sometimes with Wendy, sometimes alone or together, also made trips to the cabin almost every day, and they never went empty-handed, either. Joel and Fred began to relax, no longer hiding every time Moppa barked. Joel began spending his days carving some quite beautiful animals from scraps of wood that someone, perhaps old Gulligan himself, had left in one corner of the old cabin.

Only one thing troubled Wendy. Nimblefoot wasn't improving. No matter how often she rode him to the gulch, she couldn't get him onto the trail to the bottom, and he still stumbled with alarming frequency when they crossed rocky stretches of ground. She racked her brain, seeking an answer to the puzzle of his fear, but she found none.

On Thursday she was disappointed when the Boyds drove in just as she and Aunt Laura were clearing the lunch table. She hurried to help her aunt show them to their cabin and prepare a late luncheon for them and their ten-year-old daughter, Linda Sue. By the time they had finished, it was far too late to drive into town for the second gymkhana practice.

145

"I'm sorry about the practice," Uncle Art said as they walked down to the corral together. "I forgot all about it till just now. Why didn't you say something?"

"Aunt Laura needed me," Wendy said. "She didn't have anything ready for lunch. I mean, they said they probably wouldn't be in till after dinner, and—"

"And you're a darn good helper," he said. "Still, you need a chance to learn the other events. The gymkhana is a week from Sunday. It's just for the club members, but it isn't fair to you to have to go in with no practice at all."

"Maybe Kirk and Carol will show me what they practiced," Wendy suggested, thinking that it would be another good excuse for a private ride that could go by Gulligan Gulch.

Uncle Art nodded. "That's a good idea. Nimblefoot catches on quickly enough, so you should be able to ride in everything if they'll help you. Why don't you call and see if they'd like to come over tomorrow? You can work the horses in the big corral. You'll have enough room, with just three horses, and I think maybe Linda Sue and Jimmy

146

would get a kick out of watching."

"I'd sort of thought about practicing in the lake pasture—" Wendy began, then stopped as her uncle shook his head.

"If I remember the schedule, one of the events is the hurdles, and you'll need to do that in the corral, where we can set up the jumps."

"I'll call them tonight," Wendy said, "after they get home from practice." She opened the corral gate to let Gypsy out, her mind busy with plans for getting away to the gulch first thing in the morning.

"How are you doing with training her?" Uncle Art asked, making her forget the problems she'd been having with Jimmy, who seemed to follow her on foot whenever she rode off toward the north pasture.

"Watch this," Wendy said as she called the filly to her. "Back, Gypsy," she ordered. "Back, girl."

The filly backed away from her at a trot, going nearly a hundred feet before Wendy called her back, petting and praising her. "Isn't that wild? She loves to back up, and she goes so fast. One of these days, she's going to back into something

147

and scare herself to death."

Uncle Art laughed and shook his head. "She's an odd one," he admitted, "but that's a good thing to teach her. In fact, I think you should go ahead with her training. There's no reason why you can't start her with the training bridle and bitting rig. You won't be able to ride her for at least another year, but you could teach her to pull the old pony cart. Smart as she is, you're going to have to keep her so busy that she won't get bored and start making trouble."

"Really?" Wendy hugged the filly. "When can I start?"

"Tomorrow, when we work the young horses, I guess. There's not much to do at first; just let her get used to the feel of the bit in her mouth."

The next few days passed on wings. There were never enough hours—working with Gypsy in the morning, learning how to take Nimblefoot over the low hurdles Uncle Art had set up in the big corral, practicing the ribbon race with Carol till they could keep Quito and Nimblefoot running close enough together to hold on to the ends of the ribbon that made them a pair—then working

148

alone with Nimblefoot so that he would race into the small keyhole-shaped outline Kirk had drawn in the corral, spin on his haunches, and race out again, without stepping over the dark lines. Everything took more time than she'd planned.

There were other things, too: the ride and picnic on the beach Saturday afternoon; a barbecue and campfire Sunday evening; excursions to various parts of the ranch with the Boyds and the Websters, rides that now included an unhappy and reluctant Jimmy riding Ladybug. Her trips to the gulch were always hurried, and she couldn't help wondering if it was going to get worse when the last cabin filled with guests.

Jimmy, though riding now, was a constant thorn in her side, and all too often she felt his hostile stare following Nimblefoot as she rode with the others or practiced alone in the corral, trying to get ready for the gymkhana, which was getting ominously close. Soon only Saturday's boat trip on the lake and a picnic on Two Pine Island remained before Sunday and the gymkhana, so important for Nimblefoot.

Saturday morning, as she raced Nimblefoot

into the now rather dim keyhole outline, turned him, and raced out, Jimmy came to lean on the corral fence. Wendy endured his eyes as long as she could, then finally stopped Nimblefoot, dismounted, and walked over to him. "What's wrong, Jimmy?" she asked. "You look mad at the whole world."

"I think you're dumb," he said.

"Why?" Wendy asked, biting back a sharper reply, reminding herself that he was a guest and had to be treated properly, no matter how much she longed to just plain slap him.

"Because you won't listen to me. Nimblefoot will hurt you, Wendy. I liked him, too. Last year I wanted him for my own horse, and. . . ." His voice faltered a little. "I almost had my folks talked into buying him, and then he tried to kill me."

Wendy swallowed a sigh, knowing from past experience that arguing wouldn't help. "What happened, Jimmy?" she asked instead. "I mean, exactly what did he do?"

For a moment she thought he was going to say something unfriendly and walk off, as he usually did, but this time, he leaned on the fence and stared past her to where Nimblefoot was sniffing the corral dust.

"He didn't want to go down the trail. He acted funny—sort of danced around at first—then, when the other horses all got ahead of him, he tried to run after them. I knew he shouldn't run on the rocks, so I tried to stop him, but then he was dancing and sort of bucking. I pulled on the reins, and he reared up. I was scared he'd fall, so I let go of the reins. That's when he fell, after he came down from rearing. He sort of jumped or bucked or something, and we went off the side of the trail."

"He's never acted that way when I've ridden him," Wendy said, now more puzzled than angry.

"You've never ridden him on a narrow trail, either," Jimmy said. Something about his face made her heart skip a beat. "You always leave him and go on foot."

"What are you talking about?" Wendy asked through stiff lips.

Jimmy's smile was unpleasant. "You'll find out," he said, turning away.

152

Wendy stood staring after him until Aunt Laura came out on the front porch and called, "If you're through working your horse, do you think you could come and help me pack the food for the cookout, Wendy? There's so much to get ready."

Wendy nodded and waved, but her mind was a long way from what she was doing as she unsaddled Nimblefoot and turned him back into the corral with the other horses. There was only one trail that she'd been using regularly, a trail where Nimblefoot wouldn't go, and *it led down into Gulligan Gulch.*

12 · Ghosts of Gulligan Gulch

THE BOAT TRIP was fun, and once they reached the island, Wendy had little time to worry or wonder about Jimmy's words, for there was a great deal to be done to get the cookout ready. Sometimes she almost managed to lose herself in the fun and laughter that surrounded the fire Uncle Art had built on the beach, and the aroma of sizzling meat reminded her that she was starving.

After dinner, while the adults relaxed contentedly beside the embers of the fire, Wendy took Jimmy and Linda Sue exploring around the rocky island. They collected weirdly shaped bits of driftwood, and Jimmy found a flint arrowhead that Wendy hoped would distract him from whatever plot or plan he might have. However, as they gathered around the revived fire to toast marsh-mallows, she quickly learned that she was wrong.

"Did you know there's a haunted gulch on the Cross R?" she heard Jimmy ask Linda Sue in a low voice.

Linda Sue shook her head, and as Wendy listened from the shadows behind the two children, she heard Jimmy whispering the whole story to the wide-eyed girl. When he finished, Linda Sue shook her head rather doubtfully. "There's no such thing as a ghost," she said, but without conviction.

"I don't think so, either," Jimmy agreed. "I think there are robbers or cattle rustlers hiding in the gulch, and I'm going to find out."

"What do you mean?" Linda Sue asked.

"I'm going up there tonight. I've followed Wendy a couple of times, so I know where the path goes down, and this time, I'm going to see what she and Carol and Kirk have down there that's so interesting."

"You're going tonight?" Linda Sue looked shocked. "But it'll be getting dark before you can walk that far."

"I don't care. I've got to find out what's down

there. Do you want to come with me?"

Wendy's stomach twisted with fear. A week or ten days ago, she wouldn't have worried, for Joel and Fred would have hidden at Moppa's first warning bark, but now. . . . Moppa's greeting bark sounded every time she and Carol and Kirk made the journey to the bottom of the gulch, and Joel and Fred were usually at the end of the trail, waiting for them.

"I'm not going into any haunted gulch at night," Linda Sue said firmly. "Could we go tomorrow?"

Wendy's heart lifted at the thought that she could warn the boys, but Jimmy was already shaking his head. "It has to be tonight. Wendy knows I've seen her going down there, and she might warn the robbers."

"Wendy wouldn't help bank robbers," Linda Sue said loyally. "I think you're making the whole thing up."

"I am not." Jimmy's tone was angry and pouting. "You just wait. I'll find out who's hiding in the gulch, and you'll be sorry you didn't believe me." He got up, and Wendy just managed to duck back into the shadows before he turned around.

He stamped past her, heading for the boat, obviously planning to wait there till everyone else was ready to go home.

Wendy took her time with the packing and cleaning up of the remains of the picnic, her mind whirling with a thousand fears. She had to do something, she knew, but what? It wasn't till she was in the boat that a solution suggested itself to her.

When they reached the dock, she excused herself for a moment and ran into the diner that served the Littleville dock area and public beach. Her hand shook a little as she deposited money and dialed Carol's number. Making it as brief as possible, she explained what had happened and laid out her idea. Carol's delighted laugh was her answer.

"Kirk and I'll meet you there," Carol said. "We'll bring what we need." She was still giggling when she hung up.

"What's up?" Aunt Laura asked after Wendy had slipped between the many boxes of leftover food in the station wagon.

"Carol asked me to call her as soon as we got

157

back," Wendy said, hating herself for lying but knowing no other way to do what she had to do. "She wondered if I could ride over for a little while this evening."

"Isn't it kind of late to be riding around?" Uncle Art asked. "Nimblefoot's not a surefooted mount, and—"

"Would it be all right if I rode one of the other horses?" Wendy broke in. "Like maybe the little black that Mrs. Boyd has been using? You said he was really surefooted."

She sensed rather than saw the glance that her aunt and uncle exchanged, but she didn't take time to worry about the significance of it. All that mattered was her uncle's answer: "Well, just don't stay over there too late, now. The gymkhana is tomorrow, you know."

"Don't worry; I haven't forgotten," Wendy said, wishing that she could forget, at least for a little while. There were just too many things to worry about right now. To change the subject, she looked behind them and asked, "Where are the Boyds and Websters? They didn't drive ahead of us, did they?"

158

"They were going into town for something or other," Aunt Laura said. "I offered to bring the children back with us, but they said no, they'd all be along after while."

Wendy leaned back with a smile of relief. Her plan would never work if Jimmy got to the gulch before she did. If they were to do it, they had to be ready for his arrival.

Everything went smoothly at home. The boxes and sacks were carried in, and Wendy had time to change into riding clothes and saddle the black gelding before car lights announced the return of the Websters and the Boyds. Wendy led the gelding across Happy's paddock and out the side gate to avoid being seen by the returning guests, then mounted and loped the horse along the fence. Her heart hurt a little as she heard Gypsy's lonely whinny from the corral, but she had no time to think of missing the filly now.

Unlike Nimblefoot, the gelding, whose name was Soot, moved over the rocky ground without any hesitation, and when they reached the gulch trail, he trotted along it without objection. The only sound was the rattling of his hooves on the rocky trail. When they neared the bottom, however, the silence was broken by two whinnies, telling her that Carol and Kirk had already arrived.

"Wendy?" Carol's voice was low and cautious.

"Right here," Wendy said, sliding down. "Where are you?"

"In the brush. The boys are with us," Kirk answered. "We put the horses back near the cabin. Let me take yours, too, so they won't do any more whinnying."

Wendy handed over the reins without argument, and in the moonlight, she could see the surprise on Kirk's face as he recognized the change in horses. "No Gypsy?" he asked.

"I thought I'd better leave her home this time," Wendy said. "Her and Nimblefoot both, just in case Jimmy looks in the corral before he comes."

"You're sure he's coming?" Joel asked.

"They drove in just as I was leaving, so it'll be a little while, but I'm sure he'll come. He told Linda Sue that he was going to, so. . . ."

"Well, here's your sheet," Carol said, handing Wendy a piece of white cloth. "We decided to hide in the bushes here, then stand up when he

160

gets near the bottom. If we moan, that ought to get rid of him for good."

"I hope so," Wendy said, too weary by now to join in the excitement she sensed in the others.

"Lucky we had these sheets left from last year's Halloween party," Kirk said. "There are even eye-holes in them."

"Oh, good," Wendy said, battling her way into the folds of cloth, then wiggling it around till she located the openings. Then she settled herself on the ground behind a low bush, trying to relax for what she knew might be a long wait.

The minutes dragged by, and Wendy was conscious of the soft sounds the others made as they moved impatiently on either side of her. In the distance, she could hear the light jingle of bits and the creak of saddles as their horses moved around, grazing. It would have been very peaceful if she hadn't been so worried about the gymkhana tomorrow and the importance of it to Nimblefoot's future. If he did well, she was pretty sure that Uncle Art would be willing to give her time to work with the gelding, to solve the riddle of his behavior on rocks. But if he didn't do well—

She forced her mind away from the thought.

There was no reason why he shouldn't do well, she told herself. She had practiced hard, going over and over the maneuvers of each race, not caring whether Nimblefoot had the speed to win a ribbon but anxious for him to show that he was willing and able to do what was asked, without stumbling or getting too excited and nervous.

When she first heard the rattle of stones, she paid no attention. Then another pebble from the trail rattled down the steep slope, bringing her mind back to the present, and her eyes focused on the final turn. In a moment, a small, dark shape came slinking around the ledge, paused for a moment in the moonlight, then started down the last easy slope to the bottom. Wendy tensed, waiting, as agreed, for Kirk to make the first move.

Jimmy had just reached the bottom of the trail and stepped off onto the grass, when a low, terrible moan came from the brush at the side of the gulch. Jimmy stopped, and Wendy could see his eyes widening as the rustling in the brush began. Feeling a bit guilty, she leaned forward to shake the bush that was her own hiding place, uttering,

162

at the same time, a tremulous, frightened cry.

For a moment, the boy stood his ground, but when the first of the ghostly white shapes rose from behind the bushes, he screamed in mortal terror and set off wildly up the trail. Wendy settled back behind her bush with a sigh, her ears tuned to the sounds of sliding rock and running feet as they grew fainter and fainter.

"Well, that ought to take care of him for a while," Kirk said with satisfaction.

"I'm just glad he didn't fall off the trail," Carol said. "The way he was running. . . ."

"I didn't even think of that," Wendy admitted.

"Well, at least he's gone," Joel said, "and I don't think he'll be back for a long time."

"I'll bet he doesn't stop running till he hits his cabin door," Kirk said.

"I wouldn't, either, if I'd been him," Fred said, taking off his sheet and trying to fold it.

"Well," said Wendy, "I guess I'd better get started back. I promised Uncle Art and Aunt Laura that I wouldn't stay too late, and we sure don't want them calling your folks, Carol."

"We'd better ride out through the bottom of

the gulch so you can come home from the right direction," Carol said, "just in case your little friend raises an alarm."

"You don't think he'd do that, do you?" Wendy asked, suddenly afraid.

"I hope not," said Kirk, "but we don't want to take any chances." He turned to Joel and Fred. "You guys had better keep out of sight tomorrow, at least till you hear from us."

"Shall we leave the sheets here, just in case?" Carol suggested, and Kirk nodded.

In a few minutes, all three of them were mounted, waving good-bye to Joel and Fred, and riding along the narrow floor of the gulch beside the small stream. Since they were forced to ride single file most of the time, no one said much, and when they parted at the gate that linked the north and lake pastures, they only promised to see each other at the gymkhana, nothing more.

Wendy rode home in a frenzy of worry, but she found the house peaceful, with the Boyds, the Websters, and Linda Sue all settled in the living room, eating popcorn and watching television. She waited till a commercial, then asked softly,

"Where's Jimmy? Doesn't he like TV?"

Mrs. Webster frowned. "I think the boat ride was too much for him," she said. "He went to bed right after we got back."

"All that fresh air," Aunt Laura said with a smile. "I'm sure he'll be fine in the morning. I know he's anxious to go to the gymkhana."

"I think the fresh air got to me, too," Wendy said, yawning as convincingly as she could. "I think I'll go to bed now. Tomorrow's going to be a big day for Nimblefoot and me."

13 · Gymkhana

THOUGH SHE WENT to bed, Wendy found sleep a long time coming. She heard the Boyds and Websters leave and listened to their laughter as they walked from the main house to the cabins. She waited tensely to hear if there were further sounds from the Websters. All was quiet, however, telling her that Jimmy had returned home safely from the gulch.

Abigail, perhaps bored with the demands of her three month-old kittens, came to sleep on the bed, purring contentedly in Wendy's ear and soothing her to sleep at last. Her sleep was troubled, though, filled with ghostly shapes, running children, and horses that stumbled even on smooth ground. She woke, still weary, at dawn.

167

Breakfast was an ordeal, though Jimmy was subdued, offering none of his dire predictions about Nimblefoot's possible antics. The morning dragged along, with none of Wendy's chores really taking her mind off the upcoming events.

Uncle Art, however, seemed quite pleased. "Looks like we've got a good day for the gymkhana," he said as they fed the horses. "Not too hot but with plenty of sunshine. We should get a good crowd from town, which will help with the expenses."

"Expenses?" Wendy was surprised.

"The Saddle Club sponsors the gymkhanas, the horse shows, the Junior Rodeo, and things like that every summer, and we have to make enough money on our gate receipts and the food concessions to pay for upkeep on the arena and to make our payments on the land under it." He grinned. "The Saddle Club isn't just fun and horseback riding, Wendy. It has to be self-supporting, too, or we'd all have to pay big membership fees."

"Nothing is ever really simple, is it?" Wendy asked, her thoughts more on the boys hiding in the gulch and the troubled gelding than on the problems the Saddle Club might have.

Uncle Art laughed. "Life would be awfully dull if there were nothing to work at, no challenges to try to meet."

"It wouldn't hurt occasionally," Wendy said, picking up Nimblefoot's halter and a lead rope.

"Try not to worry," Uncle Art said gently. "He's done well in practice, hasn't he? There's no reason for his not doing exactly as well in the gymkhana."

"Will that convince you?" Wendy asked. "I mean, it will prove that he's sound, won't it?"

Uncle Art sighed. "It'll prove that there's nothing physically wrong with him," he admitted, "but it won't make him into a trail horse."

Wendy nodded. "That will take a lot more time," she said. "But does he have to be a trail horse? If he's really good in the gymkhana, couldn't he just be a gymkhana horse, at least for a while?"

That seemed to stop her uncle for a moment; then he shrugged. "Before you came to stay with us, it would have been foolish, but if you really intend to compete. . . . There are several of the young people in the Saddle Club who have horses that they use exclusively for the gymkhanas and rodeo barrel racing, so I suppose it wouldn't hurt —as long as you keep trying to cure his fear. He'll never be a complete horse with that hanging over him."

"There has to be a reason and a solution," Wendy said softly, but her heart was already lifting. Nimblefoot had been good in the practice session at the Saddle Club grounds, and she had worked him faithfully every day since. There was no reason that he wouldn't be great today.

"What about Gypsy?" Uncle Art asked as she worked over Nimblefoot's already shining black and white coat. "Do you want to take her?"

"Could I?" Wendy asked, laughing a little as the slender sorrel head came poking out of an open stall at the mention of her name. "You don't think the crowd would bother her?"

"She'll have to get used to it if she's going to be a gymkhana horse when she grows up. Besides, I thought you might want to show her in a halter class at the fair this fall. They have a Junior Showmanship event, and some of the Junior Saddle

Club members usually enter."

By the time the two horses were groomed and safely put in stalls, to keep them from rolling in the dusty corral, it was time to help Aunt Laura with lunch. Then, all too soon, Nimblefoot was making his wild leap into the horse trailer with Gypsy, and they were on their way.

The Saddle Club grounds looked very different than they had the day of the practice. Now flags and gay red, white, and blue bunting billowed colorfully in the breeze, and the rough prairie grass at the far side of the arena was nearly covered with cars. People and horses wandered everywhere, their greeting shouts and whinnies filling the air.

Uncle Art parked the pickup and trailer, then left Wendy to unload the horses and saddle Nimblefoot while he went to get her a contestant's number and a program of events. Aunt Laura, who had come in the station wagon with the Boyds and the Websters, waved as she guided the guests down to the stands, but Wendy was alone with her fears as she lowered the tail gate of the trailer and climbed up on the outside to untie

171

Nimblefoot and let him out.

The gelding bounced out calmly enough, actually seeming to enjoy the hubbub around him, but Gypsy was something else. Instead of backing out on command, she snorted fearfully and moved even farther forward in the trailer, acting as though she'd like to slink under the feedbox like a frightened dog. Wendy tied Nimblefoot and climbed into the trailer to soothe Gypsy, then slowly coaxed her into backing out.

The moment her hooves touched the ground, Gypsy scurried to Nimblefoot, pressing herself against his round side like a foal seeking comfort from its mother's nearness. Nimblefoot seemed to understand as he whickered encouragement to the filly. Wendy, her eyes on the filly, went about saddling Nimblefoot as though they were all standing around the corral at the Cross R. Uncle Art arrived just as she finished tightening the cinch.

"How's it going?" he asked, pinning the number to the back of her shirt.

"Gypsy was really scared," Wendy said, "but Nimblefoot wasn't."

172

"She looks all right now."

"What'll we do with her?" Wendy asked. "I hate to leave her up here alone. She might get scared again."

"I'll take her down by the entry pen, where we were at practice, and I'll stay with her. I think she'll be more comfortable where there are a lot of other horses and where she can see you and Nimblefoot between events. Ready to go down?"

"I guess so," Wendy said, taking a deep breath and giving Nimblefoot one final pat of encouragement before she mounted. "What's the first event?"

"The barrel-and-stake race. You'll be in the second section. Kids ten and under are first, then eleven through fifteen, then sixteen and older. Each event is set up that way so you'll have plenty of time between runs."

Wendy nodded, the knot in her stomach and the lump in her throat making anything else impossible. She felt as Gypsy must have; all she wanted was to go back to the ranch and forget the whole thing. Then she saw Kirk and Carol among the riders milling at the east end of the arena, and answered their encouraging waves.

"You ride ahead and check in through the entry gate," Uncle Art said. "We'll see you by the fence when they call your section."

"Did anything happen after you got home last night?" Carol asked as soon as Wendy reached the big corral. "Did Jimmy say anything about seeing us ghosts?"

"He hasn't said much of anything, period," Wendy said. "I think we really shook him up."

"He needed it," Kirk said without sympathy. "How's Nimblefoot?"

"A lot calmer than I am," Wendy said with a nervous giggle, then jumped as the public address system boomed out a call for the first section of the barrel-and-stake race.

"You'll be okay after the first event," Carol assured her. "Want to watch?"

The event, viewed from the entry corral, appeared simple enough. Three wooden stakes were placed in one barrel, and the rider had to race down and get them, one at a time, and carry them to the other barrel at the other end of the arena. The hard part was that they had to be picked up

174

and dropped in while the horse was at a full gallop. A large share of the stakes never made it into
the second barrel.

By the time Wendy, Carol, and Kirk rode into
the main arena, Wendy was feeling much better
and very determined. They were in the second
group of four riders to be called forward, and
Wendy found herself riding just as wildly as the
rest. She urged Nimblefoot to top speed between
the barrels and leaned perilously far out of the
saddle to drop the stakes in as he spun around for
the next run. She crossed the finish line only
inches behind Apache and well ahead of Quito
and the fourth horse in the group.

"I think we're going to win ribbons," Kirk said
as they rode off to the north to wait while the other groups made their tries. "Our times were good."

The final times proved him right; he collected
the blue ribbon and Wendy the red. Feeling ter-
ribly pleased with herself, Wendy rode over to
hand it to Uncle Art. "Isn't he wonderful?" she
said. "A real gymkhana horse!"

"You just take it a little easier," Uncle Art said.
"You don't have to win ribbons to convince me.

I just want to see that he performs without endangering you or anyone else."

"What's next?" Wendy asked, calming down a little.

"The ribbon race."

"I hope Quito will be better in that," Wendy said. "He really gets wild, doesn't he?"

"He's young," Uncle Art said. "It takes a while for them to learn. I think Carol's doing real well with him."

The ribbon race, which consisted of one circuit of the arena on a track marked by a white chalk line, was a faster event. The riders were paired, a two-foot ribbon connecting them while they raced the clock and tried to keep together so that they wouldn't be disqualified for dropping the ends of the ribbon.

Wendy and Carol managed to make the circuit together, but their time was too slow to qualify for any of the prize ribbons. Still, Wendy was feeling a strong glow of pride as she rode back into the entry corral to wait for the next event, which was to be the pole-bending.

"I think we've got some tough competition here,

176

Carol," Kirk said, riding over to join them, two ribbons now decorating Apache's bridle. He and Evan Raither had taken third in the ribbon race. "Nimblefoot's a natural at this."

"He *is* doing well," Wendy said, stroking the horse's shoulder, "and pole-bending is next, so maybe he can do even better."

Her words proved prophetic, for Nimblefoot did, indeed, excel in the twisting race through the poles. With a singing heart, Wendy rode forward to collect the blue ribbon. This proved his worth, she told herself gaily. This ribbon proved that he was meant to be a gymkhana horse, no matter what he did on the rocky trails.

The congratulations of the other Saddle Club members followed her as she rode over to where Uncle Art stood with Gypsy. The horses touched noses over the fence, and Gypsy snorted, her mismatched eyes rolling with excitement. "I think she'd like to try her luck," Uncle Art said.

"She'd probably beat us all," Wendy said. "She can really move."

"Nimblefoot's not doing so badly at moving," Uncle Art chuckled. "You're going to have the rest of the gang working harder between now and the next gymkhana. It kind of shows them up to be beaten by someone who never even saw a gymkhana before tonight."

Wendy felt herself blushing with pleasure, but she only asked, "What's next?"

"Keyhole, then the cloverleaf barrel race. The hurdles are last."

"See you later, then," Wendy said, riding back to join the others, who were watching the older kids and adults in their section of pole-bending.

"They're going to try out a new idea for the keyhole," Carol said.

"What's that?" Wendy asked.

"They always have a little trouble telling if a horse steps out of the keyhole, so this time they're going to put chalk on the whole thing instead of just outlining it; then they can see if that'll make it easier to judge," Kirk explained.

The last section of the pole-bending finished, and some of the older Saddle Club members came out to collect the poles, while others began pouring out the chalk that would form the four keyholes for the next event. They moved quickly and

178

efficiently, making it clear that this was far from their first gymkhana.

When Wendy rode out for her turn at the wild run to the keyhole, she felt more confident than ever; she even took a second look back at Uncle Art and waved. Yet the moment she touched her heels to Nimblefoot's sides, she sensed a change in the horse. He ran smoothly, easily, but there was a feeling of hesitation, even in his headlong flight. Then they reached the white pattern.

Nimblefoot skidded to a stop, his front hooves inches from the white chalk edge of the keyhole. "In, Nimblefoot," Wendy urged, kicking him a little harder as the horses on either side of her whirled into their patterns, made a cow-horse spin, and leaped out again, heading for the finish line.

The gelding reared, and she could feel his shuddering as his hooves came down inches from the white-covered earth. Rock! she realized. In his terror, Nimblefoot thought the chalk was rock. Once more she kicked his sides, trying to force him into the pattern, hoping that the proof that it wouldn't hurt him would help her later on the

179

trail. He was still shuddering.

Instead of leaping forward, Nimblefoot began backing up, not realizing that he was going to cross the keyhole in the next line. Once he did and saw the white stuff beneath his hooves, he seemed to go mad. Bucking, jumping, nearly falling, he stumbled and fled for the haven of the entry corral. Wendy clung to her perch, her heart breaking inside her. She managed to stop him once they reached the corral, sliding down to look with sorrow at the shattered horse.

Nimblefoot stood head down, trembling and panting while sweat dripped off his sides. Oblivious to the questions and offers of help from around her, Wendy began talking to the horse, doing her best to calm him.

"You'd better take him to the trailer," Uncle Art said, his voice penetrating her fog of misery. "There's a horse blanket in the tack compartment. You'll have to walk him with that on till he cools off, or he'll catch pneumonia on the ride home."

Wendy nodded, taking Gypsy's lead rope when he handed it to her.

"I'll go tell Laura you're all right," he said, "then

I'll come and help you cool him."

It was much quieter outside the arena, and the parking lot, though filled with cars, was quite deserted. Wendy plodded through it, unseeing, her mind whirling as she tried to accept and understand what had happened—and what it might mean to Nimblefoot's future.

Only when they reached the trailer did she turn back to look at the gelding. His head was still down, but the panting had stopped, and he stood quietly as she stripped off the saddle and rubbed him with a rag before putting the horse blanket over his wet body. He lifted his head and nuzzled her, pleading in his dark eyes.

"I know you're sorry," Wendy said, petting him. "So am I, but I don't know whether that will help. Uncle Art will never trust you again."

Fighting tears, she led the gelding away from the trailer, wandering among the cars, then going beyond them, Gypsy's head against one arm, Nimblefoot's against the other. She walked and walked, not thinking and not feeling anything except the ache inside her. It wasn't till she heard a distant car horn that she stopped and looked

182

around, feeling as though she were waking up.

The afternoon had grown dark and stormy while she walked, and from where she stood, she could see that the hurdles had been set up in the arena, meaning that the final event of the afternoon had begun. Heavyhearted, she turned back, heading for the pickup and trailer, knowing that Uncle Art would be there waiting to help her load the horses so they could go home.

There was no one in sight when she reached the trailer, but she heard voices from the other side. Uncle Art was talking to someone, so she stopped, not wanting to meet anyone just now.

"I completely agree, Sheriff," Uncle Art was saying. "In fact, I've thought so for years."

"Well, it's on your property," the other man said, "but I would like to check the area before we pull down the cabin. I don't believe in ghosts, but the boy's story makes me suspicious. There have been a lot of small robberies in the area lately, so someone could be hiding in Gulligan Gulch."

Wendy gulped so loudly she rather expected the two men to come around and find her, but they went on talking as Wendy listened.

"I'll have George and Cliff ready to go out there with you first thing in the morning," Uncle Art said. "The three of you should be able to tear down the cabin in a hurry; then we won't have to worry about anyone trying to use it or the kids exploring it and getting hurt."

"I'll bring a couple of deputies," the sheriff said, "so it won't be much of a job. That ought to ease the Websters' minds about their son."

"I'm sure it will, and thanks," Uncle Art said. "See you in the morning."

14 · Trapped

WENDY WAS still standing beside the trailer, too shocked to move, when Uncle Art came around. "What are you doing here?" he asked, his eyes worried. "I didn't even hear you coming."

"You . . . you were talking. . . ." Wendy felt as though she were caught in a nightmare, without hope of ever waking up.

"Seems Jimmy had a bad night last night, nightmares and stuff." His eyes narrowed. "He went up to Gulligan Gulch after he got home last night, and he says he saw something that looked like ghosts."

Wendy didn't lift her head, knowing that she couldn't meet his gaze and not tell him everything. "It's my fault for telling him that stupid story about Gulligan Gulch," she said.

"Well, don't worry about that now," he said, obviously thinking her actions were caused by what had happened in the arena. "Let's just get the horses loaded. I want to get out of here as soon as we can; it looks like a bad storm blowing in." He ran his hand along Nimblefoot's back, under the blanket, then nodded. "I guess he's cooled off enough by now."

To her surprise, Nimblefoot followed Gypsy into the trailer without his usual leap, and Wendy felt a faint flickering of hope again. Maybe he had learned, she thought. Maybe the awful scene in the arena had proved something to him. Maybe now—

"What happened out there?" Uncle Art asked, interrupting her thoughts.

"It was the chalk," Wendy said. "He thought it was rock, I guess. That's been the problem all along. He was hurt on the rocks, so he's afraid to. . . ." Her voice trailed off as she tried to think of some way to deal with the horse's problem.

"You're lucky he didn't fall with you or throw you out there," Uncle Art went on, not seeming to realize that her mind was on something else. "I'm afraid Nimblefoot is just not a safe horse for you or anyone else. I know how you feel about him, but time is only going to make it worse. I'll call Dr. James in the morning and—"

"What?" Wendy's mind finally registered her uncle's words. "What are you saying?"

"Honey, he's like a time bomb ticking away. He could explode again anytime, anywhere, and next time it might not end so well. No animal is worth your life."

"But you can't—" Wendy began, then closed her mouth as she saw Jimmy and Aunt Laura coming toward the pickup. Though she could hardly bear the pain her uncle's words had started, she couldn't plead in front of Jimmy. He was the cause of it all. If he hadn't let Nimblefoot fall. . . .

"We'll ride back with you," Aunt Laura said. "Mr. Webster can drive the station wagon home."

Jimmy stepped forward. "I told you he'd try to kill you," he said, his expression of triumph making Wendy want to slap him. "He's a mean horse."

"He's a frightened horse, and it's all your fault,

187

you little brat. You're nothing but a troublemaker, and—" She stopped herself, shocked at what she'd said.

"The sheriff didn't think so," Jimmy said, though his smirk slipped a little. "I told him there was someone in Gulligan Gulch, and he believed me. You'll see."

Wendy stared at him for a moment, words flooding her mind, crying to be screamed, but she controlled them. She got into the pickup without speaking to him again. "Could we go home, please?" she said softly, suddenly achingly tired and worried about Joel and Fred. With the sheriff coming in the morning, they would have to be warned.

The afternoon sky darkened even more as they made the slow passage out of the Saddle Club grounds. By the time they reached the ranch, the wind was raging wildly around them. Thunder crashed and lightning streaked through the black clouds, though no rain had fallen yet. Uncle Art was driving slowly, but he nearly hit the dark shape that hurtled across the road in front of the pickup, and Wendy could hear the rattle of the horses' hooves as they were jolted in the trailer.

"The horses are out!" Uncle Art shouted, not moving forward again, though the animal had vanished. He turned to Aunt Laura. "I'd better go back to the gate and wait for the Websters," he said. "You take the pickup on down and get the horses unloaded."

Aunt Laura looked as though she'd like to argue but only said, "You're going to get soaked in a few minutes."

"You can bring me a slicker if I'm not back by the time you get unhitched," he said, then got out, muttering.

"How do you suppose the horses got out?" Wendy asked her aunt, who was moving over to the driver's side of the pickup.

Aunt Laura only shook her head as she started inching the pickup along the narrow gravel road. In a moment, however, the reason became clear, for as they rolled into the open, they could see the lightning-blasted tree still smoldering in the yard. George came forward, his face black with smoke.

"You didn't hit one of the horses, did you?" he

189

asked. "They're all out there somewhere."

"Just missed one," Aunt Laura said. "What happened?"

"Lightning hit the pine, and the horses went crazy. The big roan tried to jump out and broke the top rail doing it. The rest went after her. We were so busy trying to keep the fire from spreading, we couldn't go after them." George stopped and looked around. "Where's the boss?" he asked.

"He went back to the gate to stop the Websters when they drive in." Aunt Laura looked as weary as Wendy felt.

"Let me help you unhitch the trailer," George said, "then I'll drive out and block the gate with the pickup so no one else can come in tonight."

Wendy backed the two horses out of the trailer and led them toward the barn, knowing that they couldn't go into the corrals tonight. The storm's wind shrieked, tearing at the horse blanket that still covered Nimblefoot. Thunder rolled, seeming to shake the entire earth; then the clouds cracked apart, and rain came down in sheets so thick that Wendy could scarcely see the open barn door. Though they ran the last few steps, they were all

190

drenched by the time they reached shelter.

Everything was a blur once the horses were put in stalls. It was as though someone else were helping to fix the chili and corn bread that Aunt Laura had planned for the evening meal. Someone else seemed to answer the few questions directed her way. Someone who wasn't really Wendy saw and heard and talked but didn't feel anything—just the numbness that had come over her after the keyhole race.

Only once did something touch her, and that was after the Websters and the Boyds had said good night and Uncle Art was locking up. "You know," he said, looking out at the pouring rain, "if this keeps up, the sheriff may not have much to do in the gulch tomorrow."

"What do you mean?" Wendy asked.

"Maybe the cabin will have washed away on its own."

"That's wishful thinking, Art," Aunt Laura said. "That cabin has been there a hundred years, so a little more rain won't hurt it."

"What about the horses?" Wendy asked, looking out toward the empty corrals.

191

"We'll get them in the morning," Uncle Art said. "They'll be around looking for food, I imagine." He hesitated, then added, "We'll talk about Nimblefoot then, too. You get some sleep now."

Wendy nodded obediently, turning toward her room, but once she reached it, she knew that it would be a long time before she went to bed. First, she would have to warn Joel and Fred, and to do that, she was going to have to ride Nimblefoot one more time.

It was hard sitting in her room and watching the square of light on the grass, from her aunt and uncle's window, waiting for it to be turned off so she could slip out into the wet night. She was nearly dozing by the time the light finally disappeared. Wendy dressed quickly, pulling on her warmest clothes, then reached for a waterproof jacket, though the rain had finally stopped.

The air was cold but sweet and fresh-scented as she ran across the soaked ground, skirted the burned tree, and slipped into the barn. Gypsy and Nimblefoot both whickered greetings as she passed them and felt her way into the tack room, not daring to turn on a light for fear Cliff or

George would see it. She found Nimblefoot's bridle without difficulty and hurried back, not bothering with a saddle this time.

She opened Gypsy's stall door, too, knowing that the filly's whinnying would wake everyone if she left her behind. As quietly as possible, she led the horses out into the night, mounting Nimblefoot from the broken fence rail. Sure that the gelding wouldn't do well on the rough track, and not wanting to leave him on the ridge while she walked down into the gulch, Wendy took the long way around. She headed for the open end of the gulch, knowing she could ride in that way.

When she reached the opening, however, she found that things had changed since her last trip through the gulch. The small stream that had meandered along the gulch floor was swollen from the rain and had splashed well over its banks. Wendy guided the gelding into the gulch nervously, hoping that the frail moonlight would help him find his way along the treacherous bank of the stream.

Nimblefoot lived up to his name, picking his way along the slippery ground without a stumble.

193

Gypsy followed him like a shadow, instead of bounding ahead as she sometimes did. She hesitated only once—when they reached the narrow point of the gulch and had to wade through the steadily rising water.

Wendy's relief at reaching the closed end of the canyon was brief, gone the moment she rode out of the bushes and could see the cabin—or what was left of it. "Joel! Fred!" she cried, horrified at the broken, twisted wreckage of the cabin.

"Wendy?" Fred's voice sounded very small and frightened, but Moppa's bark was filled with joy. "Over here."

"What happened?" Wendy asked, sliding off Nimblefoot and running to where Fred and Moppa were crouched on the buckled porch of the cabin. "Where's Joel?"

Fred's lips were quivering. He said nothing but pointed into the cabin, where she could see the faint light of the old lantern Kirk had brought. She made her way cautiously across the broken floor, then peered down into the blackness of a hole that had opened beneath the cabin. Joel's face was a pale blur.

194

"Wendy?" The voice was faint, but it was music to her ears. "Can you get me out of here?"

"Can't you climb out?" Wendy asked, peering down at the timbers that had fallen into the hole. "I didn't bring a rope."

"I'm under a timber, and I can't get out." Joel's voice sounded a bit stronger. "Did you ride in?"

"Yes, why?"

"Maybe if your horse could pull the timber off, I could climb out . . . if my arm isn't broken."

"I think I should go for help," Wendy said, terrified at the thought of what could happen if even one of the timbers was moved.

"There isn't time," Joel said. "Shine the light down here, and you'll see."

Wendy got the lantern and cautiously leaned over the pit to look. What she saw was horrifying. Joel was trapped beneath one of the broken timbers so that only his face, shoulders, and arms were showing, but worse, water was pouring into the pit from what appeared to be a break in the rock.

"The rain started a rockslide," Joel said. "The cabin caved in, and I slid down here with it. The water must feed the stream outside, but it's coming in faster than it can drain out. I'll be underwater in another fifteen minutes."

He was speaking matter-of-factly, but Wendy could hear the note of panic underlying his words, and she knew that he was right. "Is there a rope here?" she asked.

"Here," Fred said, edging across the slanted floor to where she knelt. "Carol brought this a few days ago."

"Can you tie it around the timber, Joel?" Wendy asked.

"I'll try. Drop the end down."

Wendy studied the coil of rope, then shook her head. "It's not going to be long enough," she said.

"What do you mean?" Fred asked. "It'll reach from here to the outside."

"But I rode in bareback," Wendy protested. "There's no way to tie it to Nimblefoot."

"Maybe we can lift it," Fred suggested without hope.

Wendy just bit her lips and stared into the pit, knowing that they could never move the huge, waterlogged timber. Then she thought of some-

196

thing. "You and Joel get the rope around the timber," she said. "I'll rig a harness for Nimblefoot."

Working feverishly, she still took nearly all the fifteen minutes to tie the heavy sheets into a rough breast strap and bellyband harness for Nimblefoot, and even when it was complete, Wendy was afraid that it would pull apart or tear when the strain was put on it. Still, she reminded herself, it was their only hope, so it would have to be tried.

She hurried back into the cabin and found that Fred had been busy, too. Using the burlap bags they had brought with them to the cabin, he had made his own rope and was now in the pit with Joel, holding his brother's head out of the steadily rising water.

Wendy closed her mouth over the doubts she had been about to voice. "The minute the timber lifts at all, pull him free," she said. "I'm not sure how long Nimblefoot can hold it up."

Fred nodded, and Wendy carried the free end of the rope out and secured it to the longest sheet, which she had tied to each side of the bellyband to distribute the strain as evenly as possible. Once it was in place, she mounted the gelding and rode

197

him forward, her nerves tightening as she felt the sheet harness pull.

Nimblefoot stopped as the cloth tightened across his chest, but she urged him ahead, wanting a slow, steady pull rather than a jerk that might break the knots or tear the cloth. For a moment, the gelding hesitated, obviously confused. "Pull, Nimblefoot," she whispered. "Just a step at a time."

She leaned forward, pressing her knees into his sides. He took a step, then another. Time seemed to stand still, and only her own fears roared in her ears. Another step, then a fourth, and suddenly they were catapulted forward as the sheet ripped. Wendy nearly bounced off over the gelding's haunches before she regained her balance. Feeling sick, she turned the gelding back and slid off.

"We made it!" Fred was shouting as she reached the door. "Help me, Wendy."

She leaned over the edge of the broken flooring, and her heart lifted again. Joel lay on top of the timber now, pale and sick but free!

"You'll have to help me get him out," Fred called. "He's hurt, Wendy."

198

15 · Gypsy Takes the Lead

IT WAS TORMENT as they tried to lift and drag the semiconscious Joel up out of the now nearly filled pit, but somehow they managed. Once he was up in the lantern light, however, Wendy felt even worse, for she could see the bruises on his head and the strange lump in his arm that made her sure it was broken.

By leading Nimblefoot up to the high end of the porch, they managed to half slide, half lift Joel aboard the patient gelding; but as he settled down astride the horse, he slumped forward, unconscious. Sick and frightened, Wendy took the rope and tied Joel's feet beneath the gelding's belly. Then, after binding the broken arm to his chest, she looped the rope around his shoulders and around the gelding's neck.

"Let's go," she said, starting back along the bottom of the gulch, the way she had come. However, they had gone only a few hundred feet, when she realized that they weren't going to make it out through the gulch. In the time they had been trying to free Joel, the stream had grown to river proportions, had risen so much that when it reached the narrow point, it would be well over Fred's head and flowing far too rapidly for them to swim.

"We'll have to take the trail out," Wendy said, leading the two horses, the boy, and the dog away from the already overflowing stream to where the grass ended at the ridge trail. With her arm around Nimblefoot's neck, she could only pray that the gelding would forget his terror of the rocky trail. She knew there would be no way out for them if he didn't—not the way the water was spreading through the gulch.

Nimblefoot moved calmly enough till his front hooves rattled on the stone of the trail. Then he stopped, trembling in terror, bouncing as though he'd stepped on hot coals instead of firm rock.

Fred whimpered a little, and Joel groaned but didn't open his eyes.

Wendy tried leading the gelding forward again, but the moment his front hooves touched the rock, he reacted the same way. "Whip him," Fred said. "Make him go."

"Not on a trail like this," Wendy said. "If he panics, he'll just fall and kill himself *and* Joel."

"Joel has to get to the doctor," Fred said, "or he might die. He said he hurt inside from where the timber was on him."

Wendy bit her lip, trying to think. Deep inside, the words "like stepping on hot coals" echoed through her mind. Then she remembered the things Jimmy had told her about the gelding's behavior on the trail, his dancing and rearing. And the way he had refused to step on the chalk . . . and what was it George had said about his shoes being nearly torn off and his hoof cut up inside? Suddenly it all seemed to move together.

"Get me the burlap sacks, Fred," Wendy said, tearing at the tattered sheet harness, which was, incredibly, still in place. In a moment she had torn a half dozen strips from it.

202

"What are you—" Fred began as he returned and saw her untying the burlap sacks.

"Just help me get these apart," she said. "It may be our only chance to get Joel out of here in time."

As soon as the first bag was free, Wendy took it and slipped it over one of Nimblefoot's front hooves. Then she wrapped the bag tight with the strips of sheet. It made a cumbersome bandage, but the gelding offered no objections.

"Do you think it'll work?" Fred asked as she fastened the fourth bag in place.

The water was creeping across the grass toward them, and Wendy could hear it roaring out from under the broken cabin. The rockslide must have blocked the spring's normal path beneath the ground, and now it was flooding wildly. If this *didn't* work, she had no doubt that they'd be drowned before Fred could reach the ranch and bring help.

"It has to," Wendy said grimly. She moved back to the horse's head and took the reins, but when she tried to lead Nimblefoot forward, he stopped at the edge of the rock, memory holding him back, even though there would now be no telltale rattle of rock under his hooves. Wendy jerked the reins, but Nimblefoot only set his feet more firmly. Tears burned in her eyes. "You've got to go, Nimblefoot," she wailed.

Gypsy's soft muzzle brushed her cheek, and for a moment, she felt the filly's warm body next to hers. Then suddenly the reins were jerked from her hands, and Gypsy's hooves rattled on the stone as she began backing up the trail. Nimblefoot trembled at the sound, but one foreleg lifted and tentatively touched the stone. Wendy moved to stand beside him but didn't speak or touch the horse as she watched him take a second step, then a third and a fourth.

"Go on ahead with Moppa," Wendy said to Fred. "Just walk past Gypsy slowly, and then run and get everyone up at the ranch. Tell Uncle Art to call the doctor. I'll stay with the horses."

The trip up the trail was a nightmare that seemed centuries long. She lived in constant terror that Gypsy would back off the trail or that the occasional rattling of pebbles and loose shale under Gypsy's hooves and her own feet would send the gelding into a panic. Neither happened.

Gypsy backed slowly and carefully, her mismatched eyes never leaving Nimblefoot's frightened brown ones, and, though Nimblefoot trembled at every sound, he never faltered or refused to move forward. Somewhere beyond the depths of his private terror, he had found trust in Gypsy and in her, Wendy realized. As they neared the top, only her worry about Joel kept her from feeling happier than she had since the gymkhana.

When they reached the final rise, Wendy's ears caught the distant sound of a car motor, and she nearly collapsed with relief when she saw the bouncing lights of the pickup. Gypsy reached the ridge, and Wendy took the reins from her, leading Nimblefoot the last few yards herself. Uncle Art and Aunt Laura were waiting in the glow of the headlights.

Though she could see the questions in their eyes, there was no time to talk as Uncle Art untied her ropes and carefully placed the unconscious boy in the back of the pickup. "I'll ride with him," Aunt Laura said. "We'll see you later, Wendy. You bring the horses down." Then they were gone, and Wendy was alone with Gypsy and Nimblefoot.

Achingly weary, she unfastened the burlap bandages, then dragged herself up onto the horse's back for the ride back to the ranch. Though the distance wasn't great, it seemed to take forever, but she didn't hurry Nimblefoot. She knew that he, too, must be feeling the effects of his trip up the ridge trail.

She took a few extra minutes in the barn with both Gypsy and Nimblefoot, then headed for the brightly lit house. To her surprise, she found only Mr. Webster sitting in the living room. He was sleepily sipping a cup of coffee.

"You all right?" he asked.

Wendy nodded. "Where's everybody?" she asked.

"Your aunt and uncle drove into town with the older boy. The other one, Fred, is up at our cabin with Jimmy." He smiled. "They seem to be making friends."

"How . . . how was Joel?" Wendy asked.

Mr. Webster shrugged. "They won't know till the doctor can examine him, but he was conscious long enough to tell Fred not to worry, so that's a good sign. Your aunt and uncle said for you to go right to bed."

"But I—" Wendy began, but Mr. Webster's gesture stopped her protests.

"They won't know anything about the boy till morning," he said, "and tomorrow could be a hard day for you, so I think you'd better take a warm bath and try to get some sleep. You're going to have a lot of questions to answer when everyone gets back."

Though she had wanted to argue, Wendy found that Mr. Webster was right. She had barely enough strength left to undress and bathe, and she was asleep almost before her head touched the pillow. Her room was full of sunlight when she opened her eyes again.

Taking time only to pull on a robe, she hurried out to the kitchen. "How's Joel?" she asked anxiously as Aunt Laura turned from the sink.

"Outside of a slight concussion, a broken arm, and a whole bunch of bruises, fine," Aunt Laura said, holding out her arms for Wendy to run into them. "Thanks to you. Fred told us all that happened at that miserable cabin."

"You saved Joel's life," Fred called from the table, where he and Jimmy were finishing off a stack of pancakes.

"After putting his life in danger by letting those boys stay down there," Uncle Art said, coming in from the garage. "I told you that cabin was dangerous, but you didn't listen."

"But you would have called the authorities, and then Moppa would have to be—" She stopped, realizing that the sheriff was behind her uncle.

"You have to learn to trust people more than that, Wendy," the sheriff said gently.

"You mean you won't send Joel and Fred away?" Wendy asked cautiously.

The sheriff sighed. "I called Missoula this morning and talked to their mother. She's been half out of her mind with worry about them."

"We didn't think she'd know," Fred said. "We wanted to write, but we were afraid she'd tell someone and. . . ." He looked at the small white dog sitting under the table. "We were just scared, that's all."

"Well, you can stop worrying," Uncle Art said

kindly. "Your mother has given permission for you two to stay here till she's out of the hospital."

"Stay here?" Fred looked stunned. "You mean it?"

"Of course, you'll be working," Uncle Art said solemnly, though Wendy could see the twinkle in his eyes. "There are lots of chores to do on a ranch, you know."

"I'll help you, Fred," Jimmy said. "If we do them together, then we'll have time to explore and ride and go swimming and. . . ."

Wendy didn't say anything. She just ran to her uncle and threw her arms around him. He hugged her tight, then said, "Don't you think you ought to get dressed and eat so we can go get the rest of the horses? Some of them didn't come back this morning."

It was nearly an hour later when Wendy led Nimblefoot out of the barn, saddled and ready to ride with Uncle Art, who was already mounted on Happy Warrior. "You know," he said, "I was halfway to town last night before I realized what I'd seen on the ridge."

"You mean Nimblefoot?" Wendy asked, her

heart pounding with excitement.

He nodded. "Want to explain?"

Wendy talked slowly, carefully explaining her theory and how the tortured climb up the ridge trail had proved it. "He must have hurt his hoof before he fell," she finished. "That's the only thing that makes sense."

Uncle Art nodded. "If he had a loose shoe and got a sharp rock caught in it somehow, that would explain his supposed bucking and the way his hoof was cut up inside. But what happened in the arena yesterday?"

"I guess the solid chalk keyhole looked like rock to him, and he thought if he steped on it, it would hurt his hoof again. That's why he stumbled on rock, too. He's trying to keep his hooves off the ground, as if it were hot."

"I still don't see how the burlap on his hooves was enough to get him to cimb that trail," Uncle Art said as he guided the Appaloosa stallion into the trees.

"It wasn't," Wendy said, leaning over to pet Gypsy's slender head as the filly trotted along beside her. "It took trust to get him up that trail. He trusted Gypsy to lead him and me to stay beside him and keep him from getting hurt again."

Uncle Art thought for a while, then nodded. "If it's the sound that bothers him, maybe George can figure out some kind of pad for his shoes," he said. "He can't wear burlap bags all the time."

"That should help till he really gets his confidence back," Wendy agreed.

"It'll take a lot of time," Uncle Art warned her. "Time and trust."

"With the new help you just hired this morning, I should have more time," Wendy said, grinning, though she could feel tears burning in her eyes. "And he deserves all the time he needs, don't you think?"

"I guess he's earned it," Uncle Art said with a smile. Then his eyes twinkled again. "Besides, I couldn't break up a friendship like that." He gestured at the two horses, who were touching noses as they paused in their search for the missing horses.

"Gypsy and Nimblefoot," Wendy said. "They're a good team."

"You're the one who made them a good team,"

Uncle Art said gently, "and I'm proud of you, in spite of your not telling us about the boys. Just remember, though, people have to trust, too, just as horses do."

"I won't forget," Wendy said, leaning forward to hug Nimblefoot's neck while Gypsy nuzzled her hair. "I'll never forget that, Uncle Art."